MIRACLE FOR A MADONNA

Lord Mere is visiting Italy to recover a valuable necklace stolen from his sister when he discovers there is much more than theft behind the jewellery's disappearance. When he meets Florencia, who is engaged to her family's long-standing enemy, Vincente de Gorizia, Lord Mere quickly realises she is desperately unhappy and marrying, against her will, a man with an unsavoury reputation. In resolving to save her, Lord Mere risks everything; at stake is a country's priceless art treasure, treason—and his own life...

Miracle For A Madonna

by
Barbara Cartland

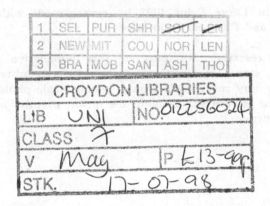
Magna Large Print Books
Long Preston, North Yorkshire,
England.

British Library Cataloguing in Publication Data.

Cartland, Barbara
   Miracle for a Madonna.

   A catalogue record for this book is
   available from the British Library

   ISBN 0-7505-1108-7

First published in Great Britain by Hutchinson, 1984

Magna Large Print is an imprint of
Library Magna Books Ltd.
Printed and bound in Great Britain by
T.J. International Ltd., Cornwall, PL28 8RW.

Author's Note

Raphael born in 1483 was one of the kindest and most gentle of the famous artists. Everyone loved him, he quarrelled with nobody. He painted many pictures of the Madonna and each one has a beauty and serenity which portrays the perfection all men seek in a woman. Few artists have been more loved and admired in their own lifetime, and after his death he was posthumously enthroned as the perfect master and 'Prince' of painters.

Paul Martin born in 1864 was the most famous pioneer of photography in England and the 'Facile' Hand Camera provided him with some of his best pictures. Made in 1889 the price was £3.3s.

Florence is still one of the treasure chests of Europe and the beauty of the city, the luridity of the light and the very human qualities of its people remain unchanged over the centuries.

1

1893

Lord Mere sat down to breakfast with a hearty appetite.

When he was in London he liked to ride early in the morning before the Park became crowded.

This morning he had been exercising a new horse he had recently bought at Tattersall's.

It was a very spirited stallion and he had innumerable tussles with it before the animal came to realise he had met his master and settled down to behave respectably.

This success had given Lord Mere, who was an outstanding horseman, a great deal of pleasure and had swept away the cobwebs of what had been a night that his contemporaries called 'one of irrepressible gaiety'.

He had however, when he had left a House of Pleasure in St James's which had been taken over for the evening by a rich Peer who was celebrating a sensational win on the Grand National, realised that he had over-indulged himself like a child let loose in a sweet-shop.

Lord Mere, who as a rule enjoyed life to the full, also had a serious side to his nature which few people realised.

He had in fact, become deeply involved in secret exchanges between France and England, and had also visited unofficially on behalf of the Government, various other countries in Europe.

Only the Foreign Secretary was aware that Lord Mere had other interests in visiting the country in question besides what appeared to be, on the surface, his endless search for pleasure.

Exceedingly good-looking, wealthy, the titled member of a family which won frequent acclaim in the history books, he had managed with some dexterity to reach the age of twenty-nine without being pressurised into marriage.

There had however been aspiring mothers pursuing him ever since he had left Eton.

Only by confining himself to the fascinations of women who were already married had he managed so far to avoid them.

His house in Park Lane, which had been built and furnished by his grandfather, was run as a bachelor household with a smoothness and expertise that he had achieved after years of studying his own comfort and in consequence other people's.

'I have always said Ingram, that you are the best host in England,' the Prince of Wales had said only a week ago when he dined at Mere House. 'I cannot think why my Chef is incapable of producing a dinner to equal yours!'

Lord Mere had acknowledged the compliment but had not elaborated on the reason for what he thought of as the perfection of his household.

Part of it was undoubtedly due to the efficiency of his secretary but, as he had learned in the Army, reform should begin at the top and he took a personal interest in even the smallest detail where it concerned himself.

He also extended his personal jurisdiction to the management of his estates with the result that his Family Seat in Buckinghamshire was a model of its kind.

His stable at Newmarket was the envy of his competitors and to their chagrin, he walked away with all the Classic Races.

As Lord Mere finished the excellent dish of lamb cutlets served with mushrooms which had arrived yesterday from his house in the country, he made a gesture to indicate that he would like another cup of coffee.

The footman who had been standing stiffly to attention behind his chair moved to obey his Master.

As he did so the door opened and the Butler announced in pontifical tones:

'The Marchioness of Kirkham, M'Lord!'

Lord Mere looked up in surprise as his sister, looking exceedingly attractive in a Spring ensemble in the fashionable shade of green, came hurrying into the Dining-Room.

As she reached the end of the table he rose to his feet saying:

'This is certainly a surprise, Jennie. I have never known you to be awake at this hour, let alone out in the fresh air!'

'I have to talk to you, Ingram!' the Marchioness said urgently.

The note in her voice and what he saw was an expression of agitation in her blue eyes made Lord Mere realise that she wished to speak to him alone.

'Will you have a cup of coffee or something to eat?' he asked.

'No, no!' the Marchioness replied. 'I want nothing!'

Lord Mere had only to look at the footman for him to know what his orders were, and he quickly left the Dining-Room by the Pantry door, closing it behind him.

Lord Mere sat back in his chair which, carved with a crown supported by angels, made him appear positively regal.

'What is the matter?' he enquired.

To his surprise his sister gave a little sob.

'Oh, Ingram, I do not know—how to—tell you!'

There was so much pain in her voice that Lord Mere reached out to take her hand and hold it comfortingly in his.

'What has upset you?' he asked. 'It is not like you, Jennie, to be "down in the dumps"!'

He smiled as he spoke remembering it was a phrase they had used to each other as children.

But his sister gave another little sob and holding tightly onto his hand with both of hers, she said:

'Oh, Ingram, if you do not help me I am—completely and—absolutely lost!'

'Tell me what is wrong!' he said quietly.

'You will be—shocked.'

'I do not think so.'

'You are the only person to whom I can turn, and oh, Ingram, I have been such a stupid fool!'

'That is something we all are at times,' he said consolingly, 'but what can you have done?'

She took her hand from his and taking a

12

lace-edged handkerchief from her belt she raised it to her eyes.

'He was so desperately—overwhelmingly —attractive,' she said, 'and I doubt if anybody could have—resisted him!'

'Resisted who?' Lord Mere asked.

The Marchioness drew a deep breath.

'Prince Antonio di Sogino.'

Lord Mere did not speak, but his eyes expressed curiosity, and there was a glint in them which those who had worked with him on some dangerous missions would have recognised.

Because it seemed that for the moment his sister was incapable of continuing he said:

'I know of whom you are speaking, but how does he concern you?'

For a moment he thought she was going to prevaricate and not tell him the truth.

Then as if she realised that he had to know exactly what had happened she replied in a very low voice.

'You know that Arthur is away in Paris at the moment?'

Lord Mere was well aware of this and

that the Queen had sent his brother-in-law to remonstrate with the British Ambassador over some small item which had incurred her displeasure.

When he heard about it he had thought at the time that Her Majesty was making a 'mountain out of a mole-hill'.

It would have been far easier to send a letter than to ask the Marquess of Kirkham, who was approaching the age of sixty, and was not in good health, to journey to Paris on her behalf.

The Queen was however so used to using him on missions which she thought of as her personal concerns that the Marquess had felt obliged to accede to her request.

'Yes, I knew he was in Paris,' Lord Mere said aloud.

There was a little pause before his sister went on:

'I met Prince Antonio about ten days ago at Marlborough House, and as he danced so divinely I found it difficult to refuse to give him the two or three dances that he begged from me.'

Looking back Lord Mere remembered

thinking that his sister was being somewhat indiscreet with the young Italian, knowing that as they made such a handsome couple on the dance-floor they would not go unnoticed.

'He begged me to let him call on me the next day,' Jennie went on, 'and when he told me how much he loved me I cannot pretend, Ingram, that I was not—fascinated by—him.'

She spoke in a very low voice without looking directly at her brother, her blue eyes lowered to the table, almost as if she was watching what had happened pass in front of her like a picture.

'I drove in the Park, I went to parties, and wherever I was he seemed to be there too.'

If his sister had been fascinated by Prince Antonio, Lord Mere could understand that he had found Jennie irresistible.

Fair-haired, blue-eyed, and with an exquisite complexion, she was an artist's dream of the 'perfect English Rose'.

He had however often regretted when he became old enough to think about it that she had been married so young to a man twenty-five years older then herself.

It had been a brilliant marriage from a social point of view.

The Marquess of Kirkham was *persona grata* at Windsor Castle and rose soon after the marriage, to the position of Master of the Horse.

He had been married when he was young, but his first wife had died in childbirth, and because he was a very distinguished widower, there was much speculation as to who his next Marchioness would be.

Then he had seen Jennifer, a young girl of eighteen, and lost his heart.

He had swept her up the aisle almost before she had time to realise what was happening or her father and mother could question whether it was wise for her to marry a man so much older than herself.

It did not seem to matter at the time, but now Jennie was thirty-four and at the height of her beauty, her husband was nearing sixty and to all intents and purposes an elderly man.

Although he could guess the end of the story Lord Mere enquired:

'Go on! Tell me what has happened.'

'Last night,' Jennie said in a voice that was barely audible, 'I gave in to Antonio's pleadings. We had dined together the night before, and somehow, I do not know how, I resisted him. I kept thinking that however—difficult Arthur might be, I was his wife and should—behave in the way he—expected me to.'

'Of course,' her brother agreed.

'Then last night we dined—alone and afterwards...'

The Marchioness stopped speaking and the colour rose in her cheeks before she said:

'You can guess what happened!'

Her brother's fingers tightened on hers.

'I can and I do understand.'

He thought to himself as he spoke that it was something he was surprised had not happened a great deal sooner.

The Marquess had not only grown pompous with age, but also sharp and dictatorial with everybody around him, especially his wife.

At the same time he was an exceedingly proud man, and Lord Mere knew that if he had the slightest idea that Jennie was unfaithful the consequences would be exceedingly unpleasant.

'I am ashamed now that I could have done—anything so—wrong,' Jennie said, 'but it is not—only that!'

'Then what else?' her brother enquired.

'Last night I wore, because I knew it would intrigue and interest him, the Florentine necklace.'

Lord Mere knew exactly to what she was referring.

Two years ago when after the birth of two daughters she had presented the Marquess with a son and heir he had bought her an exquisitely beautiful necklace.

It has been made in Italy in the first half of the 18th century, and was fashioned with a delicacy and brilliance that was typical of the Florentine Jewellers.

On a ribbon of brilliants were strung flowers fashioned of fine diamonds with leaves of emeralds.

An elaborate pendant hung from the centre of the necklace in the form of a flower from which hung two smaller pink diamond pendants.

Like all jewellery of the time it was set in silver, and each stone was held in place by a convex element which enhanced the reflection of light.

It was so lovely and so unusual that Jennie had been overwhelmed when she received it.

The Marquess had explained that it had been offered to him by the ancient Florentine family to which it belonged with the explanation that if they had to sell it, they would rather it was owned by him than by anybody else they had ever met.

He had been so flattered by the compliment that Lord Mere had always suspected he had paid more for it than it was worth, but felt it was some recompense for Jennie for having, as he knew, a husband who was growing too old to be the ardent lover she desired.

It had, in fact, surprised him that

19

unlike most of the beautiful women in the Marlborough House Set Jennie had remained faithful to the Marquess for so long.

As the fashion for promiscuity had been set by the Prince of Wales, it was accepted that the famous Beauties, after they had presented their husbands with an heir and been married for at least ten years, should have discreet love-affairs.

It was also accepted that their husbands should 'turn a blind eye' to what was happening.

Lord Mere had always suspected that if the situation in his sister's case arose the Marquess would do nothing of the sort.

In fact, he was sure that his brother-in-law would take up the attitude of a 'dog in the manger', and if he could not give his wife what she wanted, she would have to go without it.

At the same time, because he loved his sister, he would have liked to see her happy.

He had suspected for some time that Jennie was restless and frustrated though they had not discussed it, and he thought now that what had happened was inevitable.

However it was unfortunate that Jennie should have taken a foreigner as a lover.

Not that Lord Mere had anything against foreigners in principle, except that they were usually unpredictable and unlikely to offer a woman the steadfast unswerving devotion that he would have liked his sister to receive.

Now looking down at her frightened face, he realised that something was very wrong and he wondered apart from her guilty conscience what it would be.

Because she knew he was waiting, Jennie went on:

'Antonio left—at dawn. In fact, I was—worried in case the servants would be—moving about and they would—see him.'

'And when he had gone?' Lord Mere asked.

He felt certain the Marquess could not have returned at such an early hour, and he could not believe that there was anybody

21

else in the household who would accuse her of infidelity.

'When he had gone,' Jennie said in a whisper, 'although I could not believe it—my necklace had—vanished!'

There was silence as Lord Mere stared at her in sheer astonishment.

'Are you saying,' he asked after a moment, '—can you think that the Prince—stole it?'

'It has gone, vanished completely! I put it back in its box which lay on my dressing-table. Then after my maid brought me my breakfast she asked:

'"Shall I put your jewellery in the safe, M'Lady?"

'It is something she always does, and I answered:

'"Yes, of course, Rose, but be careful with the necklace!"

'It was then she opened the box, I suppose to see if the necklace was properly arranged, and exclaimed:

'"It's not here, M'Lady!"'

Now as Jennie looked up at her brother, her eyes were dark with fear.

'It had gone, and although I searched everywhere I remember absolutely clearly putting it carefully in its place and thinking as I did so how exquisite it looked against the black velvet with which the box is lined.'

'You must be mistaken!'

'No, I am not! Now, when I look back, I can remember I was wearing it the first night I met Antonio. He admired it and paid me compliments saying that of all the necks it had encircled since it was first made in 1725, mine was the most beautiful!'

Lord Mere did not speak and she went on:

'It was only this morning that I remembered the conversation and thought it strange that he knew the actual date that the necklace had been made when Arthur was not certain of it himself.'

'He might have been guessing,' Lord Mere suggested. 'What else happened?'

'After that, if I did not wear the necklace when I was at parties he always said to me:

'"Where is your Florentine necklace? I admire you in that and nothing else is beautiful enough to touch your skin."'

'So that is why you wore it last night when you were dining alone with him!'

'Yes, of course,' Jennie answered, 'and the moment he came into the Drawing-Room, before he even kissed me, he said:

'"That is how I want you to look!"

'I was slightly piqued because his eyes were on the necklace rather than on my face.'

Lord Mere stirred a little restlessly.

'That still does not prove that he stole it from you!'

'He undid it for me and as he did so kissed my neck and said:

'"You are too lovely to need such ornamentation, even anything so perfect as the necklace from my country, fashioned by my people."'

Jennie gave a little sigh.

'I was not really attending to what he was saying. I took the necklace from his hands and put it into the box. I wanted him to think of me and to talk to me.'

'You are quite certain that is where you put it?'

'Absolutely certain,' she replied. 'As I told you, I arranged it carefully because it is so precious and valuable and I am always afraid it might break and Arthur would be angry.'

She gave a cry.

'Now what can I do? Arthur will not just be angry with me, he will be outraged! How can I every explain that Antonio took it from my bedroom!'

Taking her fingers from her brother's hand she cried

'Oh, Ingram, Ingram, help me! Save me! If Arthur ever finds out what has happened he will kill me!'

'Then he must not find out,' Lord Mere said, 'and the first thing is to ask the Prince for an explanation as to what happened last night.'

'Do you suppose I have not thought of that?' Jennie asked. 'I called at the Italian Embassy where he is staying half an hour ago. I know it was indiscreet, but I was so desperate that I felt I must get in touch with him immediately.'

'What happened?'

He thought he knew the answer already.

'The servants informed me,' Jennie replied, 'that Prince Antonio di Sogino had left for Italy at eight o'clock this morning?'

Her voice broke on the last words and she put both her hands up to her eyes to hide her tears.

Lord Mere sat very still. Then after a moment he said:

'Do not cry, Jennie. I will find a way out of this mess, as long as you swear to me on the Bible that there is no possible chance that anyone else could have taken the necklace? For instance, you do not suppose a burglar could have got inside your bedroom after the Prince had left?'

'Not unless he had wings with which to climb in through the window,' Jennie replied. 'I saw Antonio out myself through the garden door, and before we went down the side staircase, you know the one I mean, I locked my bedroom door and took the key with me.'

'Why did you do that?'

'I do not know why, except that I was afraid that by some mischance my maid would come to me before I had had time to tidy away my clothes which were just thrown on the floor and of course, the—bed.'

Jennie blushed again and looked down at the table.

'So you see, nobody could have come into the room because I had the key in my hand, and after I had let Antonio out into the garden I went back, unlocked my door, tidied away my clothes, and made quite certain that everything was in its place before I went to sleep.'

'But how could he have taken the necklace without your being aware of it?'

'When he woke me saying he was leaving, and I realised how late it was, he was already dressed.'

'I see,' Lord Mere said. 'So while you were sleeping he could easily have put the necklace in his pocket without your being aware of it.'

'Of course, and I did not think about

my necklace until Rose opened the box before putting it in the safe.'

Again Jennie gave a cry.

'Oh, Ingram, suppose I had thought it was safely there, and when Arthur perhaps in two weeks time asked me to wear it, I had then found the box empty!'

'I expect that is what the Prince was hoping would happen, and it is therefore his misfortune that you discovered the loss so quickly.'

'The necklace is not there! So what can I do?' Jennie pleaded. 'You know how pleased Arthur was to give me anything so unusual, and I know it was very, very expensive.'

'I am sure it was.'

'How can I say it was a burglar when nothing else is missing?'

She paused and her brother asked sharply:

'That is true? You have checked and nothing else has gone?'

'No, nothing,' Jennie said. 'My diamond bracelet, my ring, my earrings, they were all there on the dressing-table.'

'Just the necklace!' Lord Mere said reflectively.

'Just the necklace!' Jennie agreed. 'The necklace that Arthur will never forget. Oh, Ingram, think of the scandal if he divorces me, and even if he does not do so, I know he will never, never speak to me again he will feel so affronted.'

Now the tears were running down her cheeks and she was unable to control them.

Lord Mere got to his feet.

'There is only one thing I can do.'

'What is that?' she asked miserably.

'Go to Florence and find out exactly what has happened. If that damned Italian has stolen your necklace, I will steal it back from him, or make him return it by one means or another.'

'Oh, Ingram, will you really do that?'

Jennie jumped up from her chair and flung her arms round her brother's neck.

'Only you can save me! Oh, dear, dear Ingram, you are so clever! If anybody in the world could retrieve my necklace it would be you!'

Lord Mere kissed her cheek. Then he said:

'Now listen, Jennie, I suppose you can trust your maid?'

'Rose adores me, as she always has. She has been with me for ten years.'

'Very well, swear her to secrecy.'

'I have done that already. She knows how angry Arthur would be if he discovered its loss. She would do anything to help me.'

'Very well, that is one good point in our favour,' her brother said. 'When Arthur returns you must not let him suspect for a moment that you are worried about anything or that you are frightened of what he might find out.'

There was a frown between his eyes as he concentrated on what he was thinking. Then he said:

'Husbands and wives have an instinct about each other which is almost like thought-reading. Whatever you do, you must not let Arthur read your thoughts.'

Jennie gave a little scream of horror.

'No—of course—not!'

'Very well then,' Lord Mere said, 'just be

like any loving wife would be, thrilled and delighted that her husband has returned safe and sound from Paris and who has been lost and lonely without him.'

He paused. Then he added:

'All women can act if they want to, and if you value your reputation and your good name, Jennie, you will have to act as you never had to before!'

'I will try—I really will—but it is going to be—difficult as I am so—worried!'

'Forget your worries, and if the worst comes to the worst, we may have to force open the safe ourselves and declare that somebody has got into the house unawares and taken your jewels in such a clever way that the Police will have no idea who it could be!'

'The—Police!' Jennie faltered.

She went very pale and her brother said hastily:

'We would only call them in as a last resort. It would cause complications because you would not wish to say that the last time you wore it was with the Prince. You would have to pretend that

31

you wore it on a subsequent occasion, or a big party.'

'Oh, Ingram, could we ever get away with it?' Jennie asked. 'You know that necklace is so fantastic that whenever I do go anywhere in it, everybody says it is the most beautiful thing they have ever seen!'

'I know that,' Lord Mere said irritably. 'At the same time, we have to have an alternative story if I do not succeed in getting it back for you.'

'But you must succeed, you will!' Jennie said. 'I know how clever you have been in the past, although you never talk about the things you do. But my friend Eileen, whose husband works at the Foreign Office, told me how much they all admire you and trust you to perform miracles when the Ambassadors have failed.'

'Your friend should not be so indiscreet!' her brother remarked sharply.

'But it is true, and that is why, darling, wonderful Ingram, you will succeed in saving me now. And I am far more important than any of the Kings and

Queens whom you have helped in the past.'

'I doubt if they would think so!' Lord Mere retorted. 'But, of course I will do my very best, Jennie, and while I have to leave for Florence, you will just have to pray for my success.'

'I will pray and pray!' Jennie promised. 'And if you do bring it back I will give St Anthony or whoever is the Saint of Stolen Goods, an enormous thank-offering I cannot afford!'

Lord Mere laughed.

'We shall certainly need the Saints on our side,' he said, 'because if the Prince has stolen your necklace, there must be a very good reason for it, which I am quite certain he will not admit except under extreme pressure.'

★ ★ ★ ★

When his sister had left after thanking him profusely and telling him that her whole future happiness depended on him, Lord Mere sent for his secretary.

He told Mr Barrington to make arrangements for his journey and cancel all the appointments he had made for the next few days.

Then he went upstairs to his bedroom to see his valet.

As he pulled open the drawer of his chest he found himself thinking of the words he had used to his sister—'except under extreme pressure'—and took a small revolver from its case.

It was one he had had specially made and was smaller than the more usual type. It was also so new that only a few other people owned one.

He laid it ready to be included in his suitcase together with a supply of the bullets that fitted it.

He then searched further into the drawer and found a sharp dagger not unlike a stiletto, which had a case over its shinning point, and which could be inserted at his waist or even if necessary in the top of a stocking or sock.

He reflected on how he had found it extremely useful and certainly protective

34

on other occasions.

He hoped however it would not be necessary to use his weapons, though he had the feeling that he was setting out on another daring adventure and Heaven knew what he might expect or find when he reached Florence.

His secretary made arrangements for him to catch the Boat-train that left at Noon.

It was short notice, but Mr Barrington was used to moving quickly where his master was concerned.

Lord Mere knew that in some magical way a reserved carriage on the train to Dover would be at his disposal, the best cabin on the boat would be allotted to him, and a Courier whom he would not see during the journey but who would travel with him, would engage a coupé for him on the Express Trains to Florence.

He, however, was anxious to leave Mere House rather earlier than was necessary to catch his train at Victoria Station.

His London carriage drawn by two superb horses drove him swiftly to the

Foreign Office where he asked to see the Secretary of State for Foreign Affairs.

He was ushered at once into the Earl of Roseberry's office who was obviously delighted to see him.

'My dear Mere,' he said, 'this is a surprise! You do not usually condescend to visit me. It is I who send you pleading messages begging your company!'

'I think you are being sarcastic, My Lord, and I need your help.'

'*My* help?' the Foreign Secretary exclaimed. 'That is certainly a change, as invariably I am asking for yours!'

'I agree, and as we are now on opposite sides of the table, I hope you will not fail me.'

'What can I do for you?'

'Tell me what you know about Prince Antonio di Sogino.'

The Foreign Secretary looked surprised. 'Is that all?'

'For the moment!'

'I am interested to learn why you wish to know this.'

'That, if you will forgive me, is my

36

business,' Lord Mere said. 'All I want is information.'

The Earl rang a bell and when a man appeared he said:

'Bring me the Florentine file.'

It took only a few minutes to bring in a large file which was set down in front of the Foreign Secretary.

He opened it and turned over a number of pages until he found what he sought. Then he said:

'The Soginos, as I expect you know, are one of the most important families in Florence, and the Prince who is head of the family, can trace his ancestry back to the 11th century, and never allows one to forget it!'

Lord Mere smiled, but he did not interrupt and the Earl continued:

'I have a report here which will not interest you, of a feud which has been taking place for years, one might almost say centuries, between the Soginos and their bitter enemies the Gorizias.'

He turned over a few more pages. Then he said:

'In recent times the Soginos have become extremely hard up and have been forced to sell some of their land on the outskirts of Florence. This has bitterly upset the Prince and for some reason which I cannot ascertain has intensified the feud between him and the Gorizias.'

It was such a typical story of great Italian families that Lord Mere thought it might have come out of some novelette. It did not appear to him to be of any importance with the exception of the fact that the Soginos were hard up.

That too was not unusual, but he asked:

'Do you know the eldest son, Prince Antonio?'

'Yes, I have met him at several parties, and I am also aware that whenever he is in London, Paris, or any other Capital City, he leaves a trail of broken hearts behind him.'

'He is married?' Lord Mere enquired.

'He was married, of course, when he was young. It was an arranged marriage, but I am not certain whether or not his wife is still alive. There appears to be no record of her death, but that is not to say that it has not happened.'

The Earl of Rosebery sat back in his chair and asked:

'Tell me, Mere, why you are interested.'

Lord Mere smiled and the Earl ejaculated:

'Damn you for being so secretive! But if you are investigating di Sogino on your own account, you might also do a little work for me.'

Lord Mere looked at the Foreign Secretary speculatively and he explained:

'I have a feeling that di Sogino and his family are somehow engaged in subversive activities against the Italian Monarchy. I may be wrong, but there are one or two things I have heard which do not add up but have remained in my mind like an unfinished symphony.'

Lord Mere rose to his feet.

'Thank you for what you have told me, and you know if I can be of assistance in any way, I will do my best.'

'That is all I ask,' the Earl replied, 'and as you well know, your best is always a great deal better than anybody else's.'

Lord Mere laughed.

'You flatter me!'

'I am merely preparing you for the Italian "Blarney", which can be as persuasive as that of the Irish and is far more dangerous than what the English call "plain speaking".'

He shook Lord Mere by the hand and said:

'Take care of yourself. You know you are very valuable to us, and we cannot afford to lose you.'

'I have the unmistakable feeling there is a hidden innuendo behind every word you are saying to me.'

Both men laughed as they walked towards the door.

As they reached it the Earl put his hand on Lord Mere's shoulder and said:

'I feel I should give you the warning that I give to every man I send to Italy: beware of eloquent dark eyes, and a stiletto!'

Lord Mere laughed again.

'I promise I will keep that in mind.'

He was smiling as he walked quickly down the corridors of the Foreign Office to where his carriage was waiting for him outside.

2

Lord Mere arrived in Florence and drove immediately to a Villa on the outskirts which belonged to a friend of his.

He had sent a telegram announcing his arrival and Sir Julius Cazenove was waiting for him with outstretched hands.

An elderly man, he had retired to live in Florence three years before, and as he was unmarried he was in consequence often lonely for his English friends.

'My dear Ingram!' he exclaimed. 'I cannot imagine anybody I would rather see at this moment than you!'

'It is very good of you to have me,' Lord Mere replied, 'and at such short notice.'

'Have I ever known you give anything

else?' Sir Julius smiled. 'Sit down, I have opened a bottle of very special wine which I think you will enjoy.'

A servant poured the wine into two glasses and after Lord Mere had taken a sip he said:

'It is very good, which is of course, only what I expect in your house.'

'Now tell me why you are here,' Sir Julius said, 'or is it a secret?'

Lord Mere raised his eye-brows.

'A secret?' he questioned.

'Oh, do not pretend with me, Ingram!' Sir Julius exclaimed. 'I know quite well how valuable you are to my successors in the Diplomatic world, and especially to the Foreign Office!'

He laughed before he went on:

'I also know you have an eye for a pretty face, but I cannot believe there are not plenty of those in London to interest you, and Florence is a tiresome journey.'

'I see you have it all worked out,' Lord Mere said, 'so I will agree that I have reasons for coming here, but I do not want to talk about them.'

'That is disappointing,' Sir Julius replied, 'but doubtless because here even the flowers have ears, I shall hear about it sooner or later.'

Lord Mere smiled and drank a little more wine.

'Although I am being irritatingly secretive,' he said, 'I want you to help me.'

Sir Julius threw out his hands.

'All I have is yours!' he said quoting an ancient saying of the East.

'Then first,' Lord Mere began, 'tell me what you know about the Soginos and their feud with the Gorizias.'

Sir Julius looked surprised.

'I cannot think why they should interest you, but for what it is worth, it is the usual vendetta between two families which has increased rather than decreased over the centuries! At the moment, however, almost like in a Shakespearean Play, an olive-branch has been extended.'

'In what way?'

'The daughter of the Prince di Sogino, a very attractive young woman, is to marry the Prince di Gorizia's son, an extremely unattractive young man.'

'It sounds a typical Renaissance drama.'

Lord Mere was however thinking that he had a clue as to why the necklace had been stolen from his sister.

He was well aware that an Italian girl, however important her ancestry, would require, whoever she married, a large dowry.

If it was true, as the Foreign Secretary had said, that the Soginos were hard up, the sale of the necklace would undoubtedly supply enough money to ensure that the Prince's daughter did not lack a suitor.

He did not however speak his thoughts aloud but merely said:

'You said that the Prince di Gorzia's son is unattractive. Why is that?'

'He has a reputation which is extremely unsavoury, even in Florence, which as you know allows men an unlimited freedom of lechery but insists that their women remain pure.'

'Then I am sorry for his bride.'

'As you are so interested in these two families, I am sure you would like to meet them,' Sir Julius suggested.

'I should be delighted! But I would not wish it to appear at all obvious that I am curious.'

'There is no need for that. I was, in fact, considering cancelling an engagement I have tonight to attend a party at a friend's house, where both the Princes have been invited. As there will be dancing afterwards, I am sure even if they are not included in the dinner-party, they will arrive later, with the engaged couple.'

'I should be delighted to accompany you,' Lord Mere said simply.

Sir Julius rose and walked to his desk which stood in the window from which there was a magnificent view over the City which ever since the Renaissance had been the cultural centre of Italy.

Lord Mere looked out and over the red roofs he could see the great dome of Santa Maria del Fiore and beside it the Campanile of Giotto silhouetted against the sunlit sky.

Beyond them the Arno flowed majestically beneath the bridges which crossed it.

It was so lovely that it brought to his mind the sculptors, the craftsmen, and the painters who had made Florence a treasure-chest of beauty which was the envy of every other country in the world.

Sir Julius having written a quick note, rang the bell and told a servant to have it taken immediately to the *Contessa* Mazara.

'You will like our hostess of this evening,' he said to Lord Mere. 'She is a woman of great beauty and even greater intelligence. She was widowed five years ago, and found herself mistress of one of the finest houses in Florence and the possessor of an enormous fortune.'

His voice deepened as he went on:

'She has been pursued by suitors not only, I may say, for what she possesses, but also for herself, but she has refused every one of them.'

'Why?' Lord Mere enquired.

'I think frankly she finds it more amusing to be adored by a multitude of men rather than to belong to just one. The Italians are very possessive about their women.'

Lord Mere laughed.

At the same time his thoughts went to Jennie, and he knew that the Marquess was no less possessive. If he was to save her from his anger, and perhaps some dire punishment which he could not for the moment envisage, the necklace must be found and quickly.

He was thinking aloud when he said:

'I shall look forward to this evening!'

★ ★ ★ ★

Lord Mere dressed for dinner in silence, until at last he said to his valet:

'I have something I want you to do for me, Hicks, while we are in Florence.'

The valet who had been slightly piqued at not being taken into his Master's confidence sooner, now became alert like a terrier pricking up his ears.

'Are we on a job, M'Lord?'

It was the sort of remark that Lord Mere expected from Hicks who had been with him for nearly ten years and had played his part in the many and various adventures which had been received with much appreciation at the Foreign Office.

'Frankly, the answer is "yes"!'

'Good! That's what I hoped, M'Lord, it was!'

The way the man spoke made Lord Mere look at him curiously.

'Why do you say that?'

'Because, M'Lord, I thinks you've been getting bored this last year with nothing to do except run about after the Prince of Wales and be chased by all them pretty ladies who should be at home looking after their own husbands!'

It was of course a great impertinence on Hicks' part to speak like that, but Lord Mere laughed.

From the moment he had engaged Hicks he had known that he was different from the usual run of servants and had an intelligence he would have difficulty in finding elsewhere.

For one thing, Hicks had knocked about Europe and spoke both French and Italian, not well, but well enough to understand what was being said, and to make himself understood.

He was also absolutely fearless, and as Lord Mere knew from experience was so loyal and devoted that he could trust him not only with everything he possessed, but also with his life.

'I get your point, Hicks,' he replied, 'but this is a different assignment from anything we have done before!'

'Does it concern Her Ladyship?'

Lord Mere frowned.

'Why should you ask that?'

'Because it seemed strange, M'Lord, that Her Ladyship should call so early in the morning, and immediately afterwards you gives me orders to pack for Florence.'

It was an intelligent guess such as Lord Mere expected from Hicks, and one of the reasons why he could be so useful.

But he had no intention of telling him about Jennie's loss and merely said:

'The Foreign Office has an interest in our visit.'

'Then let's hope it'll be a bit safer than the last time when Your Lordship ferreted out something they wanted to know!'

Lord Mere remembered how on that

occasion a bullet had passed within a hair's breadth of his head and it was only by a miracle he was still alive.

'This is nothing like that,' he said. 'I just want to know a few things which I think you will be able to find out for me.'

'I'm listening, M'Lord.'

'There are two noble families in Florence who interest me at the moment,' Lord Mere began, 'the Soginos and the Gorizias. Everybody knows them and they each own a large Palace at opposite ends of the City, besides of course, huge estates which need not concern us.'

He knew that Hicks was listening intently and he went on:

'I am particularly interested in finding out, which I will very likely learn myself this evening, whether Prince Antonio di Sogino has returned here from London, and where he is staying. I expect it will be in his own house, but one never knows! Most unattached young men prefer to be on their own.'

Hicks' lips twisted in a faint smile and Lord Mere knew he was thinking of the *garconnières* to which Frenchmen took their mistresses and which were supposed to be secret hiding-places unknown to everybody else.

Lord Mere let Hicks help him into his tight-fitting and exceedingly smart long-tailed coat before he added:

'I believe the Prince di Sogino's daughter has a necklace which is not unlike the one owned by Her Ladyship. Find out anything you can about it. I am sure the servants will talk if you persuade them in the usual manner.'

As he spoke Lord Mere put five gold sovereigns down on the dressing-table in a little pile.

'If that is not enough,' he remarked, 'you can always come to me for more.'

'I'll do that, M'Lord, but as Your Lordship well knows, I don't always have to pay people to find out what you wants to know!'

There was a hint of mischief in Hicks' eyes which reminded Lord Mere of his valet's proven success with women.

He 'had a way with him', as the servants

said, which ensured that if he paid for the information he extracted it with kisses.

Lord Mere knew that Hicks' particular methods of flattery and love-making were apparently irresistible.

He put a clean handkerchief into his pocket and as he walked towards the door he said:

'I am relying on you, Hicks, but do not get into any sort of trouble. Dark alleys in Florence can be dangerous to anybody who is not welcome.'

'I knows that, M'Lord,' Hicks replied, 'and you be careful too. I don't want to find m'self having to drag Your Lordship out of the river!'

Again it was an impertinence which Lord Mere would not have tolerated from any other servant in his employment.

But he did not reply and went down the stairs to where he knew Sir Julius would be waiting for him.

They drank a glass of wine before a servant announced that the carriage was at the door, and they walked together down passages hung with exquisite mirrors and pictures which Sir Julius had collected ardently ever since his retirement.

'Tomorrow,' Lord Mere said, 'you must show me your new treasures. I am sure you have added to them considerably since I was last here.'

'Fortunately for me,' replied Sir Julius, 'a large number of the old Florentine families have been forced to sell, and every time they part with something which has belonged to them for centuries they become more bitter against the Government.'

'I suppose that includes the Soginos,' Lord Mere remarked, thinking this was the sort of thing he should repeat to the Foreign Secretary.

'The Prince di Sogino is one of many who loathes the present administration,' Sir Julius answered, 'but I doubt if he is the revolutionary type. I would not say the same, however, about Vincente di Gorizia.'

'Is that the future bridegroom?'

'Yes, and after you have met him this evening you can tell me what you think of him.'

'You are making me apprehensive!' Lord Mere said jokingly.

They drove through the narrow streets of Florence which Lord Mere had always thought had a beauty and a mystery that were different from those of any other town he knew.

When they drew up outside the *Contessa*'s house there were linkmen with their lights.

The moment Lord Mere saw the great pillars outside the building and the exquisitely inlaid marble floors and painted ceilings within it, he knew he was going to enjoy himself.

Throughout his life he had been deeply affected by beauty, although it was something that had been suppressed when he was at School and seldom talked about even to his closest friends.

It was impossible to explain to men who were obsessed by horses and by the current toast of the Clubs, that he could find a picture or a sculpture more emotionally moving and more uplifting than what they worshipped.

He thought now a little cynically that the *Contessa's* possessions would be to him more interesting than her guests.

He knew however it would be a mistake to indulge himself in an ecstasy of culture before his mission was accomplished and he could find his sister's necklace.

The *Contessa* was receiving her guests against a background of lilies that made her appear like a jewel in an exotic setting.

She was certainly very beautiful with dark flashing eyes, and a Junoesque figure that was perfect in its symmetry.

The jewels she wore round her neck and in her hair were, Lord Mere realised at a quick glance, fabulous.

She held out both her hands to Sir Julius saying:

'My dear friend! It is always an inexpressible joy to welcome you to my house!'

'I hope I have not upset your arrangements by bringing Lord Mere with me,' Sir Julius said as he kissed her hand. 'He arrived unexpectedly and I wanted you to meet each other.'

The *Contessa* looked at Lord Mere and he knew that the words with which she greeted him were sincere.

He was too experienced not to know when a woman's eyes lit up at the sight of him, and he could feel the vibrations she sent out to him were an invitation on their own without the need for words.

He kissed her hand and as he did so her fingers tightened for a moment on his.

Then there were other guests behind them and they moved into one of the most beautiful rooms Lord Mere had ever seen.

'Why have I never been here before?' he asked Sir Julius.

'Because only in the last year has the *Contessa* come to live here,' he replied. 'It was closed because there was some modernisation to be done, and she was also involved after her husband's death in a Court case when one of his nephews tried to prove that it should not belong to the *Conte*'s widow during her lifetime, as he intended, but should go directly to the new head of the Mazara family.'

Lord Mere was aware that this was the type of law-suit which was common between Italians.

He was however surprised that the *Contessa* had won and the Courts had not awarded it to the new *Conte* di Mazara.

It was a family possession which he could see was not only priceless but steeped in antiquity.

He was so entranced by the pictures and statues with which the room was decorated that he ignored the dinner-guests now entering the room and who all knew Sir Julius.

He looked around him and found that everything he saw was a sheer delight.

Then a velvety voice beside him said:

'These are only a few of the things I would like to show you.'

Lord Mere turned his head to find the *Contessa* looking up at him.

She was taller than the average Italian woman but even so her head only reached to a little above his shoulder.

As he smiled down at her he thought how very attractive she was and she might in fact, have stepped out of one of the canvases which decorated the walls.

'Because tonight you are of course my Guest of Honour, having just arrived in Florence,' the *Contessa* said, 'I have changed the table so that you are seated on my right, and I should therefore be grateful if you would escort me in to dinner.'

'I should be very honoured,' Lord Mere replied, 'and I feel, because you are surrounded by such beautiful things, we already have a great deal in common.'

'That speech was not quite as pretty as I would have liked it to be.'

As the *Contessa* spoke she looked at him from under her long, dark eye-lashes, and the way her lips curved told Lord Mere exactly what she wanted him to say.

She flirted with him all through dinner with an expertise and a sophistication that he found amusing.

She was so very much a 'woman of the world' and in her own way so cultured that everything about her was, he thought, in keeping with the pictures on the walls, the paintings on the ceiling, and the exquisite 16th-century gold goblets which decorated the table.

Only in Italy, Lord Mere told himself, could one find such a wealth of antiquity, combined with good taste in how to display it.

Nothing jarred and everything was like the rhythm of music.

By the end of dinner he was beginning to forget everything but the allure of the woman beside him and his own response to her wiles.

'There will be dancing afterwards with a lot of young people and some of my friends who could not be included in the dinner-party will join us,' the *Contessa* said quietly. 'If there is an opportunity, I would like to show you my Picture Gallery and the very beautiful rooms that I have created for myself.'

There was no doubt of the innuendo behind the words and Lord Mere could only reply:

'I hope you will not forget.'

'How could I do that?' she asked.

There was again an expression in her eyes that told him very much more than her lips were saying.

A String Orchestra was now playing softly in the huge Drawing-Room where they had been received on their arrival.

Much of the furniture had been removed so that there was room for dancing.

There were windows which opened onto a terrace outside, and in the garden which Lord Mere had not noticed before there were candle-lanterns hanging from trees and shrubs creating a strange beauty and mystery.

As usual in foreign countries the gentlemen did not linger in the Dining-Room but left with the ladies, and as they reached the Drawing-Room the *Contessa* said:

'Shall we open the Ball together, My Lord? I know without being told that you dance lightly, in the same way that you ride your horses.'

'That is what I hope you will think,' Lord Mere replied.

He put his arm around her as the

Orchestra struck up a Waltz by Strauss and they swept over the polished floor, moving so smoothly that it was as if they were gliding over ice.

He felt the *Contessa* move a little closer to him and he knew that her eyes seeking his held an unmistakable invitation in them.

Then he heard the Major Domo announce from the door:

'*Il Principe di Gorizia.*'

The *Contessa* moved from Lord Mere's arms and hurried to greet her guests.

He heard her chattering to them in her own language and was aware that while she was talking to the thick-set, high-nosed elderly man, he was joined by a younger one.

Lord Mere was sure this was his son, Prince Vincente di Gorizia, who was to marry the Prince di Sogino's daughter.

After what Sir Julius had said about him, he looked so exactly as he had expected, that it was almost ludicrous.

Slightly hunched even at his age, he was dark and swarthy, and there were signs of debauchery about his face that were startling.

In fact, Lord Mere decided, the young Prince was repulsive, and there was no other word for it.

Because he knew it was important for him to meet him, Lord Mere walked deliberately up to the new comers to stand just behind his hostess.

They were immediately conscious of his presence and the *Contessa* said:

'Allow me to introduce to Your Highness our Guest of Honour for this evening, who has just arrived to stay with my dear friend Sir Julius. May I present Lord Mere, *Il Principe di Gorizia!*'

'Welcome to Florence!' the Prince said genially.

'I am delighted to be back!' Lord Mere replied.

'You have been here before?'

'Several times. And twelve months ago I was in Rome.'

'The Eternal City to outsiders,' the Prince replied, 'but which to us has become an overcrowded, overwhelming seat of Bureaucracy!'

He spoke scathingly and Lord Mere replied:

'It is still very beautiful!'

He thought the Prince metaphorically shook his head, then at that moment before he could speak the Major Domo announced in stentorian tones:

'*Il Principe di Sogino, e La Principessa Florencia di Sogino!*'

Extremely interested, Lord Mere saw a tall, distinguished white-haired man, whose aristocratic features might have been sculpted by Michelangelo, walk towards the *Contessa*.

He had a dignity and pride in his bearing which seemed to emanate from him so strongly that Lord Mere felt nobody could mistake him for anything but an aristocrat.

Then as the Prince bent his head to kiss the hand of the *Contessa* Lord Mere saw the girl standing behind him.

He had expected somebody attractive with dark hair like her brother Antonio.

To his surprise, however, the Princess

63

Florencia had pale gold hair and he felt he had seen her somewhere before.

Then a moment later the *Contessa* having welcomed them said:

'Florencia, may I introduce Lord Mere who has just arrived from England.'

It was then as Florencia looked at him that Lord Mere knew where he had seen her.

Not in person, but in pictures painted by Raphael, whose exquisite portrayals of the Virgin Mary he had always deeply and devoutly admired.

He saw the same perfect oval face, the same small pointed chin, the same look of innocence and purity, the same large eyes transparently clear as a summer sky.

For the moment he was bemused by her beauty, then as she gave him a faint smile Lord Mere saw she was afraid and in need of protection.

He was not certain how he knew this, and yet it was all quite clear in his mind.

He took her hand in his and thought, although he felt he must be mistaken, that as their fingers touched a little tremor ran through her.

The *Contessa* was talking to the Prince, and Florencia said in a soft voice that seemed to Lord Mere to be like the music he had heard in his dreams:

'I have always longed to visit England!'

'You have? Why?'

His eyes were on her face, and it was hard for some reason he could not define, to understand what she was saying.

'I have always thought of it as such a happy land, a place where people are content and have no wish to do anything but live at peace with their neighbours.'

He knew she was thinking of the feuds and vendettas which raged between so many Italian families and which in particular had affected hers.

'I think that is true,' Lord Mere replied. 'But you live in one of the most beautiful Cities in the world!'

'Beauty, the beauty we all long for and seek,' Florencia said, 'should be in our hearts.'

They were words that Lord Mere had

never heard spoken by so young a girl.

He was aware as she spoke that her eyes flickered for a moment towards Vincente Gorizia.

As soon as he had arrived he had gone to talk animatedly to a lady who had rushed towards him the moment after he had been greeted by the *Contessa,* and had drawn him aside as if she had something special to say to him.

Now, as if he was suddenly aware who was present, Vincente turned round and came towards Florencia saying as he reached her:

'You did not meet me today, as you said you would!'

He spoke sharply and his voice seemed to grate on the air between them.

It suddenly struck Lord Mere that if Florencia was beautiful and it would be difficult to find anybody more lovely, then Vincente Gorizia was everything that was ugly and distasteful.

'I...I am sorry,' Florencia said softly, 'but Papa wanted me at home, and I therefore stayed with him.'

'Excuses! Excuses!' Vincente Gorizia exclaimed. 'It is surprising, Florencia, that you do not run out of them!'

She did not reply to him, but merely looked unhappy and Lord Mere found himself instinctively wanting to strike the young man for upsetting anything as lovely as the girl who stood by him.

It was impossible for him to say anything, but as if what he was feeling transmitted itself to the Italian he said rudely:

'I suppose, like all your race, My Lord, you have come to Florence looking for what you can take back to your own country. I am sure you will not be disappointed. There are quite a number of people ready to sell their birth-right for a few golden guineas!'

He spoke contemptuously in a way that was like a challenge, and Lord Mere was aware that Florencia seemed suddenly to go pale.

She turned her head as if she could not bear to look at him.

'I assure you,' Lord Mere replied, 'I have come to Florence with no more ulterior motive than to see my old friend Sir Julius, and to enjoy the company of his delightful friends.'

He spoke so pleasantly that he saw Florencia look at him with what he thought was an expression of gratitude in her large eyes.

But the Prince made a sound that was little less than a snort and turning on his heel he walked back towards the lady to whom he had previously been speaking.

An ill-mannered young boor, Lord Mere thought, then heard Florencia say softly:

'I...I am sorry.'

'There is no reason for you to apologise.'

'But there is! I do not want you to have a bad impression on your first night in Florence.'

'I assure you, my only impression is that I am overwhelmed by the beauty of what I am seeing,' Lord Mere said.

He looked at her intently as he spoke and because she understood the compliment behind the words a faint flush crept into Florencia's cheeks.

Lord Mere had a sudden fear that he

might be forced to leave her and he said quickly:

'Will you dance with me?'

The question took her by surprise and she looked at her father as if for his approval, only to find that he was deeply engrossed in conversation with the *Contessa* and they had been joined by the Prince di Gorizia.

It appeared to be a subject that absorbed them completely and without waiting for Florencia's reply, Lord Mere put his arm around her and drew her onto the dance-floor.

Now the spirited Waltz had changed to a softer, more romantic one.

Because Florencia was so small and light, Lord Mere felt as if he held in his arms something so ethereal that she could not really be human.

He had danced with and made love to so many women, and they were so much a part of his existence that he could not imagine life without them.

And yet as he touched Florencia he knew there was something different about her,

69

something so strange that he could not analyse it or understand it. He only knew for certain that it was there.

They danced in silence until as they reached the far end of the room Lord Mere drew Florencia off the dance-floor and out through one of the open windows onto the terrace outside.

It was a warm night without a breath of wind and they walked down the white marble steps into the garden.

'How pretty this is!' Florencia said. 'But...perhaps I ought not to come here with...you.'

'Why not?' Lord Mere asked.

'It may be a mistake and Papa will tell me it is something I...should not do.'

'I find in life that it is always best to do what one wants and apologise for it afterwards.'

Instead of a light laugh, such as he would have received from the women he knew in London, he realised that like a child, Florencia took what he said seriously.

'That sounds very easy,' she said, 'but

70

you are a man and the sins men commit are always forgiven more easily than if one is a woman.'

This was true, and Lord Mere said:

'I promise I will not spoil your reputation or anything else about you that is so beautiful. We will stay in the light of the lanterns so that everybody can see us. But I want to talk to you, and it is difficult to do so when we are dancing.'

'What do you want to talk to me about?'

'Yourself!'

She gave a little laugh.

'That is rather dull. I would much rather you told me about England.'

It struck Lord Mere that any other woman would have said "about you", but he replied:

'What do you want to know?'

There was a little silence. Then she said:

'I think really that because I am afraid I like to think and speak of places that are safe.'

Lord Mere had stopped in the light of a

large lantern hanging from a tree covered with blossom and the light revealed the expression in Forencia's eyes as if it was daylight.

For a moment they just looked at each other. Then he said:

'We have only just met, but I think you are aware that I want to help you. Tell me why you are afraid.'

She drew in her breath and he knew that what he had said meant something to her.

She clasped her fingers together before she answered:

'I..cannot speak of it..not to a..stranger!'

'Am I a stranger?'

As he asked the question and knew she did not know how to answer him, he said:

'The minute you came into the room I knew I had seen you before. We have not met, but your face has been with me ever since I can remember. Raphael has painted you more than a dozen times three hundred years ago, and I suppose I always knew that one day I would find you.'

There was silence and Florencia's eyes were held by his. Then in a voice he could hardly hear she whispered:

'H.how can you..say this to me?'

'I can say it because it is true!'

'I should not..be listening.'

'Why not? We have met, and I am sure it was decreed that we should do so.'

She put out a hand as if she would touch him, then drew it back.

'Please,' she said. 'You are frightening.. me, though in a different way from how I was frightened before.'

'I think,' Lord Mere said very slowly, 'that I was sent by fate or the gods, or perhaps the angels, to Florence to help you. You may choose to send me away because as you say truthfully we are strangers, but I believe we are something very different.'

'I want to believe you,' Florencia said, 'and although there is no..logical reason for it..I trust you.'

'Thank you, that is what I wanted you to say. Trust me and know that I have been sent like a messenger from the gods

73

to take away your fear.'

'Nobody can do that,' she said quickly.

'How can you be so sure? We are dealing not with ordinary human problems but with something far more fundamental.'

He did not know why he said those words, but they seemed to come spontaneously to his lips and he saw her eyes light up as if she understood.

It made her immeasurably more beautiful even than she had been before, and with a faint smile on her lips she said:

'In all the books I have read, help has always come at the very last moment..when the Princess is..rescued.'

'That is what I am telling you,' Lord Mere said. 'I am here to rescue you and all you have to do is show me the Dragon.'

She gave a little laugh that had something child-like about it before she said:

'You make it sound so easy! If only it were possible!'

'It is possible, and you have to believe me.'

'I do..but I am still afraid. St George, St Michael and all the angels would find it..impossible to help me!'

'I may not be an angel, but I am always at your service!' Lord Mere said gallantly.

Her lips parted and there was a sudden radiance on her face that made her again infinitely more lovely than she had been a moment before.

Then as they looked at each other and it seemed to Lord Mere that words were unnecessary, since he was already fighting an enemy on her behalf who had to be annihilated, a voice harsh and angry interrupted them.

'So here you are!' Vincente Gorizia exclaimed. 'Your father was asking what had happened to you and why we have not danced together. Surely you are aware that it is important we should be seen doing so?'

He spoke in Italian in an angry tone which seemed to vibrate through the air, roughly dispersing the magic which had held Florencia and Lord Mere close in such an inexplicable way, and turning even the beauty of the night into something ugly.

75

Florencia lowered her eyes and said humbly:

'I..I am sorry..Vincente.'

'So you should be!' he replied. 'You know everything has been planned for tonight. We will confirm all the rumours that have been circulating about the *reprochement* between our two families. It is typical of the Soginos to be so casual about anything so important!'

Lord Mere was aware that Florencia gave a little shudder as if she expected from the way the Prince spoke that the feud between them was starting up all over again.

'Come on!' he added. 'Walk back with me, and for God's sake look as if you are enjoying being with a Gorizia, as of course I am enjoying being with you!'

There was such a sarcastic note in his voice that Lord Mere longed to hit him.

Instead he stood quietly in the background, finding it incredible that the Prince could ignore him in a manner that was so rude and at the same time so uncouth that he was not quite certain if it was

76

intentional, or simply because he knew no better.

As Florencia would have moved away from him he said:

'Let me thank you, Princess, for a most delightful dance. It has been a very great pleasure to meet you, and I promise I will not forget the things we have discussed.'

She gave him a quick glance and he knew the fear was back once again in her eyes as she turned to walk quickly after the young Italian who was already moving back towards the house.

As she reached his side he held out his arm and she put her hand inside it.

They walked up the steps and onto the terrace, and while Lord Mere watched them, his lips were pressed into a tight line.

Then he was aware that he was clenching his fists so tightly that he could feel the sharpness of his nails digging into the palms of his hands.

'Blast the young swine!' he muttered beneath his breath.

But he knew he had taken the first steps

in his efforts to unravel the puzzle.

He found it stranger, more complex and certainly more mysterious than even he had anticipated.

3

Lord Mere waited a little time. Then he walked back into the Ball Room.

A number of couples were dancing round to the music which he thought was pleasantly melodious.

The older people were sitting around the room on comfortable chairs and sofas watching them.

With a quick glance, Lord Mere saw that the Prince di Sogino was talking to another elderly man who was standing beside a superb marble statue which seemed in some way to accentuate the Prince's aristocratic features.

Lord Mere made his way towards him, aware as he did so that the *Contessa* was watching him.

Without looking in her direction he reached the Prince to stand patiently at his side until he had finished his conversation.

Then the Prince turned to him with a faint smile and Lord Mere said:

'I heard before I left London, Your Highness, what magnificent treasures you have in your *Palazzo*. Would it be very presumptuous of me to ask if during the short time I am in Florence I could visit you?'

'But of course!' the Prince replied. 'It would be an honour and a great pleasure and I can only hope you will not be disappointed.'

Lord Mere laughed.

'I do not think I could ever be disappointed in the treasures of Florence, and of course your family has been collectors for so many centuries that I know you have a treasure-trove that is famous the world over.'

'You flatter me!' the Prince said. 'I hope I may welcome both you and Sir Julius with whom you are staying tomorrow at, shall we say, three o'clock?'

'I am sure Sir Julius will find that convenient,' Lord Mere answered, 'and thank you.'

He was introduced to the aristocrat with whom the Prince was talking, then with a respectful bow he moved away.

Once again he was aware that if he looked at her there would be an invitation in the *Contessa*'s eyes.

Instead he sought Sir Julius who was sitting down on a sofa.

As he approached him the lady to whom he had been talking was invited to dance and Sir Julius was alone.

Lord Mere then bent down to say in a low voice:

'Will you say that you are feeling somewhat indisposed and wish to return home?'

Just for a moment there was a look of surprise in Sir Julius's face. Then as he had served for many years in the Diplomatic Service he merely replied:

'Of course! Now, or a little later?'

'A little later,' Lord Mere replied and

walked away across the room towards the *Contessa.*

She smiled as he reached her side in a way that told him without words exactly what she was hoping and expecting.

He sat down beside her and proceeded to pay her the compliments that had no need to be exaggerated because she was indeed a very beautiful woman.

She was just getting to the point of inviting him, as she had suggested before, to visit the Picture Gallery and her private rooms when Sir Julius interrupted them.

'Forgive me, my dear Ingram,' he said, 'but I am feeling somewhat fatigued. I feel I should go home but of course if you wish to stay, the carriage will return for you.'

Lord Mere jumped to his feet.

'No, of course not,' he said. 'You told me before we left that you were not feeling particularly well, and I only hope this delightful evening has not been too much for you.'

'I am afraid I am getting old,' Sir Julius answered shaking his head somewhat dolefully.

The *Contessa* gave a cry of protest.

'Of course you are not old!' she exclaimed. 'And I cannot lose you both so soon in the evening! Please, have a glass of champagne. I am sure it will make you feel better.'

'You must not tempt him,' Lord Mere said. 'I know what instructions his doctor has given him, and we must obey them.'

He slipped his arm through Sir Julius's and said:

'Actually by London hours it is long past my bedtime and so tonight, at any rate, we will not take any risks.'

His eyes met the *Contessa*'s as he spoke and he knew that she thought he was promising her there would be other nights and other occasions when they would meet.

Both he and Sir Julius kissed her hand and Lord Mere was very conscious that her fingers tightened on his and he heard her say very softly:

'I shall see you again?'

'As soon as it is possible,' he replied and hurried after his host to help him into his carriage.

As they drove away Sir Julius asked:

'Now, what is all this about? As it happens, I was only too willing to leave as I do find such parties extremely tiring if they go on for too long.'

Lord Mere told him the truth.

'Quite frankly I thought it would be a mistake to become too closely embroiled with our hostess.'

Sir Julius laughed.

'She is a very determined woman, and you will find it hard to escape her. Every man in Florence is aware of that.'

Lord Mere was not listening. Instead he said:

'Tell me about the Soginos and the Gorizias. How is it possible that a coarse, unpleasant young man should marry anything so exquisite as the Princess?'

'You are only voicing what everybody in Florence is asking,' Sir Julius replied. 'I know you are aware that the two families have been at each other's throats for generations. Now quite suddenly the news comes almost like a bombshell and the

83

betrothal party will take place next week.'

'But why? That is what I am asking.'

Sir Julius was silent for a moment. Then he said:

'There must of course be some reason, if not on the surface, but I cannot find an answer to your question which in fact all Florence wishes to know.'

Thinking of how Prince Antonio had stolen the necklace from his sister, Lord Mere said tentatively:

'Are the Soginos hard up?'

'Everybody says they are short of money,' Sir Julius replied, 'but di Sogino has always been thought of as a rich man. He certainly has a remarkable collection of pictures. In fact they far exceed anything owned by the Gorizias.'

'That reminds me,' Lord Mere said. 'I arranged with the Prince that you and I will visit him tomorrow afternoon at three o'clock, as I am very anxious to see his treasures.'

'They will certainly delight you.'

Again there was silence. Then Lord Mere asked:

'Surely if the Prince needs money he can sell one of his pictures?'

'That might be easy to do if he was an Englishman or a Frenchman,' Sir Julius answered, 'but the Sogino collection is part of the wonders of Florence and the people look upon it as belonging to them. There would, I am quite certain, be an outburst of indignation if any of them left the City.'

Lord Mere supposed therefore that because he badly needed money the Prince had sold the necklace to the Marquess of Kirkham with the intention of retrieving it at the first convenient opportunity.

It seemed an extraordinary thing to do, and yet there seemed to be no other explanation for the fact that in the first place the Prince should have sold anything that was so much a part of the family history, or that he should, if indeed he was aware of it, have allowed his son to be nothing more than a common thief.

The more Lord Mere thought about the Prince with his aristocratic appearance and proud bearing, the more he was certain there was more behind what had happened than what so far he had been able to surmise.

He however thought it would be a mistake to say too much to Sir Julius, and he turned his attention to the Gorizias, saying again how repulsive he found the young prince while his father looked both coarse and unpleasant.

'I have never liked the youngster myself,' Sir Julius agreed, 'and there are some unpleasant tales of his licentious behaviour that can hardly be dismissed as "boyish pranks".'

'And what are his particular vices?' Lord Mere asked.

What Sir Julius told him was so revolting and degrading that even in the darkness of the carriage Lord Mere turned to look at his host with a startled expression in his eyes.

'If that is true,' he said, 'then why in the name of Heaven does the Prince di Sogino consent to the engagement?'

Sir Julius made an expressive gesture with his hands.

'I cannot pretend to understand,' he admitted, 'but then I have found that the Italian code when it comes to vendettas and points of honour is well beyond the comprehension of any plain-thinking Englishman.'

Lord Mere laughed.

At the same time, he could see in front of his eyes Florencia's beautiful face, so like the Madonnas by Raphael that he felt as if her intrinsic purity radiated from her.

Then again he could see the fear in her eyes.

'There must be some very strange reason for this union,' he murmured beneath his breath.

He knew as the carriage drew up outside Sir Julius's Villa that he would never rest until he found out what it was.

★ ★ ★ ★

The following day Lord Mere spent the morning in the sunshine in the garden.

The view beneath him was exquisite, so

radiant with light, that his mind dwelt for some time on the City of such architectural beauty, grandeur and due proportions that at the time of its building it was a revelation to the whole of Europe.

Then, as if it was inevitable, he found himself thinking once again of Florencia, and trying to decide which of the many exquisite Madonnas by Raphael she most resembled.

He thought perhaps it was the *'Madonna of Foligno'* and yet there was an undoubted resemblance to several other Madonnas which he had studied so often in his preoccupation with Raphael as an artist.

Then Sir Julius joined him and they sat talking of their diplomatic and political friends until it was time for luncheon.

After a delicious meal served with some excellent wine the carriage was brought to the door and with the hood down they drove through the City and along the side of the River Arno to reach the *Palazzo* Sogino.

As they drove through the crowded streets, each one having a characteristic beauty that was somehow inescapable, Lord Mere felt as if he was setting out on a voyage of discovery in which he was far more personally concerned than usual.

He knew because he was honest with himself that every time he thought of Florencia he was vividly aware of the fear in her eyes after Prince Vincente had spoken to her.

And he had known too that her whole body shrank from him.

It was impossible not to envisage that nothing could be more cruel, more horrifying, than for a pure and, he was certain, innocent young girl, to be subjected to the excesses and the depths of depravity which he now knew the Prince enjoyed.

Excesses so unspeakable as to shock any man with any feelings of decency.

The *Palazzo* when they reached it, was exactly as Lord Mere might have expected.

Very impressive, partially surrounded by an ancient wall, and with trees protecting its garden from the elements.

Nearby he saw an imposing medieval

building with feudal battlements, which he was to learn later had been built in the 13th Century.

Inside there was a huge open courtyard and from the windows of the magnificent room into which they were shown there was a view over the countryside that was breathtaking.

A few minutes after they arrived the Prince came hurrying into the room and was quite obviously delighted to see them.

'My dear Sir Julius,' he said clasping his hand, 'it is far too long since you honoured me with your presence. I can only be grateful to our guest that he has brought you here today.'

Sir Julius smiled.

'I really was confined to my Villa for most of the Winter,' he said, 'but it is delightful to see your *Palazzo* looking even lovelier than the last time I was here.'

'That is what I want you to think,' the Prince replied.

Lord Mere thought however there was just a shadow over his eyes, although he could not be sure.

They drank a glass of wine, then while Sir Julius said he would rather sit comfortably than join their tour of inspection, the Prince and Lord Mere set off together.

Every room in the *Palazzo* was filled with magnificent pieces of furniture that had been handed down through the ages.

But it was not until they reached the rooms which Lord Mere learned were seldom used by the family that he came upon the collection of pictures.

They were wonderfully impressive, hanging on walls that seemed to have been designed precisely as a background for them, and they were lit by the long oval-topped windows which let in the lucid light that was so particularly Italian.

Lord Mere enthused over a painting by Leonardo da Vinci and was spellbound by a masterpiece by Giorgione.

Then as the Prince would have drawn his attention to a picture on the other side of the room he saw one by Raphael.

It was a picture he had always wanted to see of the Madonna and Child, which was known as the *'Ansidei Madonna'*.

He was standing in front of it thinking once again that there was a distinct resemblance in the downcast eyes and the soft, innocent lips to that of the Prince's daughter when some sixth sense, some intuition which never misled him told him the picture was a fake.

For a moment he could not believe it possible.

Yet, because Raphael's works meant so much to him and because, in some way he could not understand, they vibrated towards him so that he was aware of them as if they were human, he knew he was not mistaken.

His common sense told him that in this case he must be wrong. Yet his appreciation of beauty was so acute that he knew his instinct was right.

The picture was a fake and certainly had not been painted by Raphael, although he was well aware it was one of the most valued of all the pictures in the whole *Palazzo*.

He did not say anything, he only stood

before it, trying to see whether the actual brush work was different from what he would recognise as Raphael's.

Then he knew that behind him the Prince was worried by his scrutiny, and he could feel his restlessness, even while he was standing quite still.

For a long time Lord Mere did not move, then he turned and walked across the room to view the picture of which the Prince had already spoken.

He was almost certain as he did so that the Prince gave a sigh of relief, almost as if he had been afraid that Lord Mere might have expressed his doubt as to the authenticity of the 'Raphael'.

There were more pictures in other rooms, all of them outstanding, all of them, as Sir Julius had said, part of the glory of Florence.

While Lord Mere wandered from one to the other he knew the majority of them were authentic and what they purported to be, while he was absolutely convinced that the *Ansidei Madonna* was false.

He felt that a number of the smaller

pictures he looked at were suspicious, but they were not of the importance of the one he had noticed first, nor did they have the same impact upon him.

This was because he knew they were not painted by Raphael to whom he felt so personally attuned, and he told himself even in a bad light he would have been aware that something was wrong.

Their tour of the *Palazzo* was coming to an end and he was beginning to think that he and Sir Julius would leave without seeing Florencia when unexpectedly she came towards them down the passage, looking, Lord Mere thought, as if she had just stepped down from one of the pictures on the walls.

Because she had made such an impression on him the previous evening, he was apprehensive in case in the daylight she would not seem so beautiful as she had the evening before.

And yet he knew as she moved towards him that only Raphael could have painted her as she was, and the vibrations she sent out were the same as those he felt when he stood in front of one of Raphael's perfect Madonnas.

'Oh, here you are Florencia!' the Prince exclaimed. 'I forgot to tell you that I had two distinguished visitors this afternoon, and I have been afraid you might miss them.'

As he spoke the words that were ordinary and commonplace enough, Lord Mere knew, again with a perception that never failed him, that the Prince was lying.

He had deliberately not told his daughter that he and Sir Julius were coming to inspect the pictures and, although it was hard to understand the reason for such deception, the Prince was undoubtedly disconcerted by his daughter's appearance.

'Yes, I am here, Papa,' Florencia said lightly.

She held out her hand to Lord Mere.

As he took it he felt her fingers tremble just as they had last night.

He saw too that deep in her eyes the same fear was there, and his whole being cried out once again that he must help her.

'Have you been enjoying our pictures?' she asked.

'They are magnificent!' Lord Mere replied, 'and I particularly enjoyed seeing for the first time the *'Ansidei Madonna'* of which I have heard so often.'

He spoke deliberately and saw, as he expected, just a faint flicker in Florencia's eyes which told him that she knew, just as he did, that it was a fake.

Sir Julius was waiting for them in the room where they had left him.

When Florencia greeted him it was obvious to Lord Mere that they were expected to leave as the Prince offered no invitation to them to stay.

Then as he and Sir Julius walked ahead towards the stairs that led them down to the courtyard, Lord Mere hung back.

He made an excuse to study a metal-point of the Madonna and Child which hung in the passage.

He stopped in front of it and said quietly to Florencia:

'It is very like you!'

She smiled.

'That is what Papa has said, but it is difficult for me to judge.'

'But not for me.'

Then as he realised the Prince and Sir Julius were out of earshot he said:

'When can I see you? You know we have a great deal to say to each other.'

'It is impossible...quite impossible!' Florencia said quickly.

'But why? I want to see you!'

Almost as if he compelled her to do so she raised her eyes to his and he thought as he had last night that she was pleading for his help, and yet at the same time was aware there was nothing he could do.

'I must see you!'

She shook her head, but he persisted.

'There must be some way?'

She made a little gesture with her hand that was somehow pathetic and he said:

'When I saw you I thought you were too beautiful to be real, and now I know that living here amongst these pictures you have gained a beauty that is not vouchsafed to other women.'

She drew in her breath as if his words

moved her. Then she said:

'If only I could..creep back onto the..wall and stay there. Then I would be..safe!'

'If you did it would be a terrible waste of life.'

He knew as he spoke that he had said the wrong thing.

A shadow passed over her face which was very eloquent and she said in a voice which he had not heard her use before:

'It is sometimes..easier to..die than it is..to live!'

He glanced at her and at that moment the Prince was aware that they had not followed him and he called her name.

'Florencia!'

It seemed to echo along the long corridor with its arches and painted ceiling, and guiltily Florencia replied:

'I am..coming, Papa!'

She started to walk quickly and Lord Mere could do nothing but walk along beside her.

Only as they reached the top of the steps to see below them Sir Julius stepping into the carriage, did Lord Mere say:

'Do not give up hope. Just trust me.'

For a moment he saw a sudden light in her eyes as if the sunshine was caught in them.

Then the fear was back, and although she did not speak he knew she was telling him, from her heart, that it was hopeless.

As he touched her hand Lord Mere knew that their vibrations were joined for a moment, and that just as he felt there was something inevitable about their meeting, and nothing could have prevented it, so Florencia felt the same and just for one fleeting second her fingers clung to his.

Then as her eyes fell and she looked again so unbelievably like a Raphael Madonna, he said goodbye to the Prince and stepped into the carriage.

Only as they drove off did he have the extraordinary feeling that Florencia was not standing in the courtyard of her father's *Palazzo* but alone on top of a tree-less hill and the only thing beside her was an empty cross.

★ ★ ★ ★

Back at the Villa, while Sir Julius retired to his room to rest, Lord Mere sent for Hicks.

He came in with an air which told his master that he had something to impart, and closed the door carefully behind him.

'Well, Hicks?' Lord Mere asked.

He sat down on the edge of the bed as he spoke and Hicks came nearer to him, lowering his voice as he said:

'I've found out some of the things Your Lordship wanted to know.'

'What are they?'

'First, M'Lord, about that necklace. There seems to be some mystery about it.'

'What sort of mystery?'

'Well, M'Lord, one of the maids at the Sogino Palace—an' a pretty little bit her be too!—tells me it seems to have vanished in the last two years and no one's seen sight nor sound o' it!'

Hicks looked at his master, but Lord Mere only remarked:

'Go on!'

'Then I learns, and perhaps this'll surprise you M'Lord, the Prince an' his family be pushed for money, and there's been all sorts of economies made in the Palace. There's also talk of 'em selling things.'

It was what Lord Mere expected and he only nodded as Hicks continued:

'Her weren't certain what had been sold, but she'd heard the older servants talking.'

'Is that all?'

'All for the moment, M'Lord. But I'll be meeting her again. Very keen, her be, and she likes Englishmen!'

Hicks preened himself a little, and Lord Mere said:

'Well done, Hicks! But I asked you to find out if Prince Antonio had returned to Italy.'

'I haven't forgot that,' Hicks said quickly. 'He's acoming back tonight; at least, they thinks so, and he'll be staying at the Palace.'

'Thank you, Hicks! That is exactly what I wanted to know. Now when you see this girl again tonight while I am at dinner, find out which room the Prince will occupy.'

There was a faint smile on Hicks' lips as if it pleased him to think of seeing the girl again so soon.

'I'll not fail you, M'Lord.'

'As soon as you know,' Lord Mere instructed, 'come and tell me, whatever time of night you get back. Do you understand?'

'Yes, M'Lord!'

Lord Mere changed his clothes for something more comfortable, and once again went and sat in the garden.

But now he found it difficult to be entranced even with the sun setting on the spires and towers below him, or shimmering with all the colours of an artist's palette on the waters of the Arno.

Instead, all he could see was Florencia's eyes pleading with him for help, as a child might turn instinctively to somebody older and wiser than herself.

He knew without being told that she was desperate.

He knew that every nerve in her body

revolted against what appeared to be her fate, which would not only affect her sensitivity, but also her mind and the purity of her soul.

He asked himself how he knew so much, and knew it was in the same way as a Raphael portrait could draw him and hold him.

Just as it spoke to him as it had spoken to the artist who created it, so he knew just as if they had been close to each other for years rather than for only a few minutes of time that Florencia was appealing to his perceptiveness and understanding.

Because he had a professional method and expertise when he was undertaking what he thought of as 'a job', Lord Mere thought over very carefully everything he knew about the Soginos and the Gorizias.

He analysed everything he had seen and heard, everything that had made him suspicious that the *'Ansidei Madonna'* was a fake.

But at the end of the summary the questions he had asked himself were still the same, still unanswered, still a strange puzzle that he could not unravel.

He sat in the garden until the sun had set, when he knew it was time for him to have a bath and change for dinner.

He saw as he sat down with his host to another excellent meal that Sir Julius looked tired.

So as soon as they had finished he rose from his chair and said to his host:

'I fear that our excursion to the *Palazzo* and the gaieties of last night have proved too much for you. I therefore suggest that you go to bed.'

'I would like to do that,' Sir Julius said gratefully. 'At the same time, I feel rather remiss that I am not entertaining you better.'

'I assure you I am perfectly content and have no desire to do anything but read a good book and think of those magnificent pictures I saw this afternoon.'

'I knew they would please you.'

Lord Mere did not reply and after a moment Sir Julius said:

'I wish you could do something to help that wretched child! How can she face

104

marriage to a man who is a byword for depravity?'

'I have asked myself the same question,' Lord Mere replied, 'and there seems to be no answer—unless you have one?'

'I wish to God that I had!' Sir Julius exclaimed. 'I have known Florencia since she was ten years old, and every year she has grown more lovely! How can the Prince do anything so unspeakable to his only daughter?'

'He must have some very compelling reason!' Lord Mere said slowly.

Sir Julius looked at him and it was obvious that he was startled.

'You do not think—you are not imagining he is being blackmailed?' he asked hesitatingly after a moment.

'By the Gorizias?' Lord Mere finished. 'I would not be surprised!'

As he spoke he was thinking of how the Earl of Rosebery had told him that there were rumours that the Prince di Sogino was against the Monarchy.

If this was true the Prince di Gorizia might have turned it to his advantage.

And yet such an idea seemed incredible!

Lord Mere was aware that Sir Julius was watching his face. Then he said very quietly:

'I think, Ingram, if anybody can find a solution to this problem, it could only be you!'

★ ★ ★ ★

Lord Mere retired to bed at about eleven o'clock.

He did not ring for Hicks because he knew the other servants in the Villa would expect his valet to be already in his room waiting for him.

Finding him not there, Lord Mere knew that he had not yet returned from the mission on which he had sent him.

He therefore undressed and got into bed, trying to concentrate on a rather boring political study that had just been published and which he felt duty-bound to read, although it gave him no pleasure.

But he found that Florencia's lovely face kept imposing itself on the text, and he found himself thinking that he would like to see again the metal-point Madonna on the wall of the *Palazzo,* and imprint it on his mind so that he would always remember her.

Then he knew with a somewhat cynical twist to his lips that it would be impossible for him ever to forget her, and there was really no need for metal-points or paintings.

She was there beside him, haunting him whether he liked it or not for the rest of his life.

It was nearly midnight and he was still deep in thought when the door opened and Hicks came in.

It only needed one glance at the valet's face to know that he not only had the information he required, but also that he had enjoyed himself.

He walked towards the bed and Lord Mere sat up to ask:

'What have you found out for me?'

'Prince Antonio, M'Lord, is expected this evening. He should be at home by now.'

'Good! Did you find out which rooms he occupies?'

'Yes, M'Lord!'

Hicks explained exactly where it was, and Lord Mere realised that the window looked out over the magnificent view he had seen from the room in which they had been received, but was one floor higher.

There was, he learned from Hicks, a balcony to both windows of the room, and that there were balconies outside the majority of the rooms on that floor.

Lord Mere got out of bed.

'Thank you, Hicks. Now we had better hurry!'

'We're going there tonight, M'Lord?'

'Yes! You remembered to pack my usual clothes, as I asked you to do?'

'Yes, M'Lord.'

Less than twenty minutes later Lord Mere and Hicks, both riding horses from Sir Julius's stables, left the Villa.

A yawning groom, while surprised that His Lordship should wish to go riding so late, accepted the explanation that he could not get to sleep.

Hicks made the story sound even more convincing by pointing out that the moonlight made it easy for them to find their way about without there being any danger.

The streets were empty and, as Hicks had said, the moonlight was very bright, and it took them only a short time to reach the *Palazzo*.

It looked even more impressive and magnificent by moonlight than it had in the daytime.

Lord Mere and Hicks rode between the trees that encircled the formal garden until they were opposite the part of the *Palazzo* where Prince Antonio's bedroom was situated.

As Hicks pointed out which room it was, Lord Mere could see there was a light in the window.

'Wait here, Hicks,' he commanded, 'so that I shall know where to find you when I return.'

'Take care, M'Lord!' Hicks warned, speaking for the first time since they had left the Villa. 'You can't trust them

"Dagos" when it comes to fighting, and even their teeth are sharp as stilettos!'

Lord Mere did not reply.

He turned and walked away, keeping in the shadows where it was unlikely that anybody in the *Palazzo* would see him.

He was wearing a special suit he had had designed for the sort of operation in which he was now engaged.

It fitted him tightly and there no parts of it likely to catch when climbing a tree, or, as he intended at the moment, the wall of a *Palazzo*.

His shoes were soft-soled which made it easy for him to move silently and also to climb without slipping.

Climbing the walls of the *Palazzo* was, as he had thought it might be when he had seen it earlier today, very easy.

The stones were old and in many places the plaster between them had worn thin or crumbled away.

There was also on the lower floor a variety of heraldic carved shields which made perfect footholds.

Fit and athletic, Lord Mere found no

difficulty at all in climbing up the lower walls almost as if he was a spider.

Only when he reached the balcony did he move more cautiously, being careful to make no sound.

There was still a light in the room and the casement window was open to the night although the curtains were pulled across it.

With the poise and balance of a man perfectly adjusted to what he was doing Lord Mere, calculating every movement of his body, climbed through the open window into the room.

There he stood behind the curtains listening, and was almost certain there was somebody in the bed.

He thought he could hear the sound of breathing and felt that to confront Prince Antonio at such a moment with the theft of his sister's necklace would put him at a disadvantage from which he would find it difficult to extricate himself.

Lord Mere drew in his breath, almost as if he drew on a force greater than himself to give him the power to do what he had to do.

Then with a sharp movement that had something almost theatrical about it, he pulled back the curtains with both his hands.

It was a large room, and almost directly opposite him there was a huge carved bed, heavy with velvet curtains falling from a carved corola that reached almost to the ceiling.

But in the centre of it, sitting up against the high pillows, Lord Mere saw not Prince Antonio, as he had expected, but Florencia staring at him wide-eyed in sheer astonishment.

4

For a moment Lord Mere and Florencia stared at each other in sheer astonishment.

Then he recovered first and managed to say quite convincingly:

'I told you that I had to see you.'

'How could you have..got here?' she asked, then gave a little cry. 'You must have..climbed up the..walls!'

He smiled, pulled the curtains to behind him and came towards the bed.

'You might have..killed yourself!' she gasped.

'I assure you I was quite safe.'

He stood by the bed looking at her, then thinking she might be embarrassed if he sat down on it he pulled up a chair.

'Y.you should not be..here,' she said in a trembling voice.

'I know that,' he answered, 'but we are alone, and no one is aware of it, so let us talk frankly.'

He felt as he spoke that she was hardly listening but only staring at him so that her eyes seemed almost to fill her face.

Then she said quietly:

'It was..brave of you..but you should..go away.'

'I think,' Lord Mere said, 'that you would be disappointed if I left when for once we can talk to each other without being interrupted. There is so much I want to hear, so do not let us waste any time troubling ourselves about things that are unnecessary.'

She gave a little smile which he had not expected. Then she said:

'It is..difficult to know what to say..in the circumstances.'

'Not really,' he replied. 'I think you are as aware as I am that something strange has passed between us, and I know as I have never known anything so positively in my life before that I have to help you.'

A little shiver ran through her and he knew his words had brought to her mind Prince Vincente.

He thought as he looked at her that he had never seen a woman look so lovely in bed, and yet at the same time so pure and innocent.

With her long golden hair falling over her shoulders almost to her waist and her child-like nightgown trimmed with a row of lace, buttoning to the neck, she looked much as Mary must have looked when the Archangel Gabriel appeared to her.

There was, Lord Mere thought, something about Florencia that he had never encountered in any other woman, and he knew it was a purity of mind and body that was almost sacred.

Then he said very softly:

'Trust me.'

'How can..I?' Florencia asked. 'Even if I..told you what was happening, there is..nothing you could..do about it.'

'How can you be so sure of that?'

She looked at him and he felt as if she was peering deep beneath the surface.

He knew it was what he did when he was trying to understand another person, digging deep into their personality in an effort to discover the truth.

He did not speak but his eyes held hers until she said, a little shyly, as if she spoke to herself:

'H.how can you be so..different?'

'That is what I want you to think,' he replied. 'We know we are both different in a way that would be inexplicable to any ordinary person, so perhaps together we can work the miracle that is needed.'

115

He saw a sudden light come into her eyes as if that was what she had been praying for.

She clasped her hands together on the lace-edged sheet in front of her, and he saw that her fingers were very long and thin, and so beautiful that he knew that any artist would long to paint them.

He was waiting for an answer and after a moment she said in a very small voice:

'I..I do not..know where to begin.'

It was then, suddenly, like an explosion, there was the sound of a man's voice outside the room.

He was speaking in Italian and as Lord Mere started to his feet Florencia gasped:

'It is my..brother! He must not..find you..here!'

Lord Mere did not answer.

He quickly walked across the room, and knowing he had only a second or two to spare went behind the curtain of another window from the one by which he had entered the room.

He had only just drawn the curtains

close behind him when the door opened and he heard Florencia exclaim:

'Antonio! I wondered what had happened as you were so late!'

'I did not expect to find you here!' her brother answered. 'It was kind of you to wait up for me.'

'Where have you been? Papa expected you back hours ago!'

'Yes, I know,' Prince Antonio replied.

As he spoke Lord Mere heard him put something heavy down on the floor, and a second later there was the sound of somebody else, he supposed a servant, bringing in more luggage.

'That will be all, Georgio,' the Prince said.

'Shall I tell your valet that you want him, Your Highness?'

'No, I will put myself to bed.'

The servant said goodnight and went from the room, and Lord Mere knew that the Prince had sat down on the chair by the bed that he had just vacated.

'I suppose you have been worried,' the Prince said.

'You have it with you?' Florencia asked very softly.

'Yes, I have brought the necklace back with me,' Antonio replied. 'One of the reasons I am so late is because I stopped at Ponte Vecchio to give it to Giovanni, as one of the stones was loose.'

'None of them are lost?'

'No, they are all there and Giovanni says that since he last saw it it has doubled in value!'

There was silence and Lord Mere knew perceptively that Florencia was looking unhappy.

'It is no use, dearest,' the Prince said roughly. 'There is nothing we can do but let them have it, and a lot of good may it do them!'

'B.but..they want..me too!'

The words came falteringly from Florencia's lips as if she could not prevent them from doing so.

'I know, I know!' the Prince said irritably, 'but we have been through all this before, and I can think of no other way of saving Papa.'

There was silence. Then as if Florencia suddenly remembered Lord Mere was in the room she said:

'I..I suppose you want to..come to bed?'

Her brother smiled.

'You look very comfortable, so I will not move you. We can change places in the morning.'

'I only came here,' Florencia explained, 'because I was so frightened I might miss you if you went out early in the morning before I was awake.'

The Prince laughed.

'That would be a change from coming in late after you are asleep. Bianca asked me to stay with her, but I knew you would all be expecting me to be here for breakfast and so I refused.'

'You have seen Bianca?'

'She missed me as much as you have,' the Prince replied, 'and she also had information I wanted.'

'What was that?'

'A report on a few more of the disgusting things that devil Vincente has been doing in the town. I am making a list of them!'

119

'Why?'

'It may do us no good. At the same time, it might come in useful, one never knows!'

'C.could we..is it possible..' Florencia stammered, 'to..use it against him so that I need not..marry him?'

Her brother shook his head.

'I doubt it. Everybody knows what he is like and deplores his behaviour, but he is not doing anything criminal from the point of the law.'

There was a hopeless note in his voice as Prince Antonio said in a different tone:

'Oh, God, Florencia, you know I would save you if I could! But short of killing him, what the hell can I do?'

'I know, Antonio dear, but if you did that you would be hanged, and that would bring shame upon our family and I know it would..kill Papa to lose you.'

'It will kill him anyway to lose you.'

Florencia did not answer and after a moment he said more quietly:

'I can see you are tired. Go to sleep, my dearest, and go on praying until the very last moment that a miracle will save us all. There is nobody else but God to whom we can appeal.'

'I have prayed and prayed,' Florencia said with a little break in her voice, 'but I do not think He hears me.'

Her brother bent down and kissed her cheek.

'At least we have the necklace,' he said, 'which will lift one burden from Papa's mind.'

'It was very brave of you to get it back,' Florencia said. 'Goodnight, Antonio.'

'Goodnight, my dearest sister,' the Prince replied, 'and God keep you.'

He walked across the room and Lord Mere thought he picked up one of the cases which the servant had put down.

Then he went from the room closing the door behind him, and there was the sound of footsteps going down the passage.

Lord Mere did not move, knowing that it would be a mistake in such circumstances to be too precipitate.

Then he heard Florencia say in a frightened little voice:

121

'Are you..still..there?'

He came from behind the curtains and saw her staring at him anxiously, her face very pale, and he realised she was even more frightened and agitated than when he had left her.

He walked towards the bed and this time he sat down on the side of it, knowing it important that they should not be overheard, and that voices, however soft, can sound quite loud in the stillness of the night.

For a moment they just looked at each other. Then he said:

'Now there need be no pretence between us. Tell me why your brother had to steal the necklace from my sister for your father to give to the Gorizias.'

As if what he said was a shock Florencia put her hand up to her mouth as if to prevent herself from giving a cry.

Then she said in a whisper:

'I had no idea it was your..sister who had the..necklace! I only knew it had been sold to a very important English nobleman.'

'Who by an extraordinary coincidence

is married to my sister,' Lord Mere said. 'But how, Florencia, could your father sell anything so beautiful and so much a part of your history?'

She looked away from him and twisted her long fingers together before she said: 'I can..trust..you?'

He knew how important the question was to her and he reached out to take her hand in his.

He could feel that she was trembling all over and her fingers seemed to flutter in his like a little bird caught in a net.

'I swear to you before God that you can not only trust me,' he said, 'but that I will somehow save you from marrying Prince Vincente!'

As he spoke she was very still, but there was a light on her face that seemed to come from within her.

'Could you..do that?'

'I can try, and I have the feeling I shall succeed.'

'If you do..then my prayers will be.. answered.'

'But first you have to help me because I

need to know the truth—the whole truth!'
Lord Mere said softly.

He did not take his hand away from hers
knowing that she found it comforting, and
somehow because he was touching her she
was able to begin hesitatingly:

'I..expect you know there has been
a..vendetta between our family and the
Gorizias for..centuries?'

'Yes, I heard that.'

'It is something that Antonio and I used
to laugh at because it was so old-fashioned
and out of date in modern times.'

She gave what was almost a sob before
she added:

'But we..laughed too soon..and perhaps
it was our laughter..and the..jokes we
made about Vincente which made him..
determined to have his..revenge.'

'What did he do?' Lord Mere asked.

'He has blackmailed Papa!'

'How?'

There was a little pause and he knew
that Florencia was feeling for words before
she said:

'You know that since King Umberto

came to the throne many people are dissatisfied with his Government and with him?'

'I have heard that,' Lord Mere admitted.

'It is rumoured that there have been more than a few conspiring against..him, and one man..in particular whose name is..Orsini.'

Lord Mere nodded.

'I have heard of him.'

'He is powerful, but has been forced into hiding because those who support the King are determined to bring him to..justice for a number of..different crimes.'

Lord Mere was listening intently, remembering this was what the Earl of Rosebery had told him he suspected was happening.

'I know now,' Florencia went on, 'that the Gorizias must have worked hand-in-glove with Orsini, but we can never..prove it.'

'Why not?'

'Because they have been far too clever and have in fact incriminated Papa.'

Lord Mere moved a little nearer to her,

still keeping his hand over hers.

'Go on,' he said softly.

'Papa had a letter from a man he used to know, telling him that he was in great trouble and asking Papa if he would meet him in a part of the grounds where they could not be seen by anybody in the *Palazzo*. Papa thought it strange, but he has never refused to help anybody in distress, especially an old friend.'

'So he went to the meeting-place alone?' Lord Mere questioned.

'Yes, it said in the letter he must come alone, so he walked through the garden to a clearing in the woods that was very secluded and where the man was waiting for him.'

'Did your father know him?'

'No, it was not the man he expected to see, but the man who was there said his friend was too ill to come himself and he had brought Papa a special letter from him.'

'Your father did not think that strange?'

'No, he said the man in the wood seemed honest and loyal and spoke with a certain amount of authority. He therefore promised that he would help an old friend in distress in any way he could. He shook hands with the man and came back to the *Palazzo* with the letter.'

'Is that all?'

'No..no..there is much more..than that.'

'Tell me.'

'The man who met Papa in the wood was Orsini!'

Lord Mere looked puzzled.

'I do not understand.'

'Why should you?' Florencia asked. 'You could not guess any more than Papa could that while they were talking, Vincente, or one of his accomplices was taking photographs of Papa with the man for whom all those guarding the King were searching!'

Lord Mere sat upright and stared at Florencia.

Now he began to understand what had seemed so incomprehensible.

He was aware of course that photography had suddenly been launched as an exciting new invention, and in England Paul Martin had taken some fantastic publicity pictures.

He had bought for himself one of the Facile Cameras which had caused a revolution in the Printing World, but this was the first time he had realised how useful photography could be to blackmailers.

'When, a few days later, Vincente arranged to see Papa and showed him the photographs that had been taken, he could not believe what had happend!' Florencia said in a broken little voice. 'There was one of Papa shaking hands with Orsini, and another with Orsini handing him the letter from his supposed friend—that could look as if he was handing over money—and several others of them talking earnestly together.'

There was no need for Florencia to elaborate further.

Lord Mere was aware that if those photographs of the Prince were shown to the King and those responsible for his safety, there would be little or nothing the Prince could say in his own defence.

'And your father had no idea who it was he had met in the woods?' he asked.

'Not until Vincente told him.'

'Then what happened?'

'Vincente demanded an enormous sum of money from Papa as the price of silence and his promise not to show the photographs to the King!'

'So that was why your father had to sell the *"Ansidei Madonna"!'* Lord Mere said beneath his breath.

'You knew..it was a..fake?'

'I was sure of it.'

'How could..you know? It was copied by..one of the greatest artists alive, a man to be..trusted because Papa had helped him when he was poor and..struggling.'

'I agree it is a magnificent painting,' Lord Mere conceded, 'but there is something lacking.'

'What is that?' Florencia asked curiously.

'I cannot explain exactly, but because I especially love Raphael's works they vibrate to me in the same way that you and I vibrate to each other.'

He spoke quite quietly, but her eyes fell before his, and the colour flooded into her pale face.

She looked so lovely that he had an irresistible desire to bend forward and kiss her.

He knew however that this was something he must not do, and instead his fingers tightened over her hands as he said:

'Go on. I am sure that having compelled your father to pay once, he made him pay again and again.'

'Vincente demanded more and more money.. and while we feel sure that..some of it goes to..Orsini..'

She stopped and added hesitatingly:

'..the rest goes towards his pleasures.. which I understand are..very expensive.'

There were tears in her eyes as she went on:

'Papa has not dared to sell another picture except for two smaller and less important ones..in case anybody should become..aware of what he has been..doing. If people ask questions..the whole story.. will come out.'

'I can understand that,' Lord Mere said sympatheically.

'At last..when there seemed to be.. nothing left..Vincente said papa must give him the necklace..having no idea that we had already sold it.'

Tears ran down her cheeks as she said:

'Selling it added..ten years to Papa's age. The necklace has been in our family..ever since it was made more than a century and a half ago.'

'The money kept Vincente quiet?' Lord Mere asked.

'Only for a short while. Then when Papa said there was nothing more he could give he laughed and replied:

'"Florencia is now eighteen. What could be more suitable than for her to marry me?"'

Lord Mere saw the expression on Florencia's face which told him how deeply she had been shocked.

'I could not..believe Papa when he told me..what had been proposed,' she whispered after a moment. 'I knew it was not because..Vincente wanted me as a..woman.. but because it was his..ultimate revenge upon the Soginos.'

Lord Mere was silent simply because he did not know what he could say.

Yet he could understand the twisted way in which Prince Vincente's mind was working.

'On top of..that,' Florencia went on, 'Vincente demanded that the necklace, which the Gorizias have always coveted, should be part of the marriage dowry.'

'And your father could not admit that he had sold it.'

'Of course not. Nobody knew that except for the Jeweller, Giovanni, who is a personal friend and would never betray us.'

'So that is why your brother had to steal it back from my sister!'

'Exactly! But please..please understand that Antonio would never normally..stoop to anything so..dishonourable, but it was a case of..saving Papa.'

She looked up at Lord Mere piteously as if afraid he was condemning her brother for what she knew he must think of as a serious crime.

'Of course I understand,' he replied.

'Now that you have told me the whole story, Florencia, I must begin to think of what I can do to save you and of course your father also.'

'Can you do..that? Can you..really do..it?' she asked.

There was an irrepressible and momentary joy in her voice. Then in a very different tone she said:

'But..I am asking..too much! How can.. anybody save us from those fiends? They have the photographs..indisputable evidence that Papa talked to Orsini..clasped his hand, and took..a package from him which could so easily be misconstrued into..something very..incriminating!'

'I have thought of all that,' Lord Mere said quietly. 'Now tell me, Florencia, when did your father last see the photographs?'

• 'When Vincente showed the prints to him and he could hardly believe that he was not dreaming!'

'And of course the negatives will be in a safe place!'

'Very safe,' Florencia said, 'as he assured me only last week.'

133

'What exactly did he say?' Lord Mere asked sharply.

Florencia turned her face away from him as if she was embarrassed, and her voice was very low as she replied:

'I..begged Vincente not to..force me into marriage I told him I..hated him..for what he had..done to my father..and it would be..impossible for us ever to find any.. h.happiness together.'

She gave a little sob as if the memory of how she had pleaded with the Prince was still vivid in her mind, and Lord Mere saw the tears run down her cheeks.

'"You will have..the necklace," I said. "You can also have the other things from Papa's *Palazzo,* if you want them..but do not..make me..marry you."'

Her voice broke on the last words, and it was impossible for her to go on.

Then as she knew Lord Mere was waiting, with a superhuman effort she managed to say:

'He seemed to listen..seriously as I spoke, and I thought for..one moment he was going..to agree. Then he..laughed!

134

It was..horrible the way he..laughed!'

Lord Mere's fingers tightened on her hands as if to comfort her.

'What did he say?' he asked.

'He said: "You will always do exactly what I want because in a safe in my bedroom there is indisputable proof that your father is a traitor to his country and his King!"'

As Florencia spoke the last word she took her hands from Lord Mere's and put them up over her face.

As if he could not help himself, he put his arms around her and drew her close to him so that she was crying against his shoulder.

'It is all right,' he said. 'Do not cry. Now that I know what I am up against, nothing is impossible.'

She was still for a moment. Then she raised her face to his to look up at him.

The tears were still wet on her cheeks and on her dark long eye-lashes as she said:

'You are..not suggesting..that you climb into the Gorizias' *Palazzo* as you did ours?

135

No..no! You cannot do..such a..thing!'

'Why not?'

'Because it would be dangerous..terribly dangerous! They have many more servants than we have..and if Vincente found you there..he would..k.kill you.'

'I am not afraid.'

'But..I am afraid! How can I let you..die for us?'

'For you,' Lord Mere said very softly.

He looked down at her, her eyes were held by his, and very slowly and gently, as if it was something ordained since the beginning of time, his lips found hers.

He felt the little quiver that went through her, then the softness of her mouth still trembling from her tears brought him a rapture he had never known before in his whole life.

It was far more than the joining of their lips. It was as if the vibrations from them both were linked together, and his heart touched her heart, his soul hers.

For a long moment their kiss was sacred and almost inhuman.

Then as Lord Mere felt her surrender

herself to him, his arms tightened around her and his lips became more demanding, more insistent.

A flame rose within them both that was so ecstatic, so perfect, that he knew it was something he had been seeking all his life and thought he would never find.

Never in any one of his love affairs when he had been deeply attracted, enthralled and enraptured by the woman to whom he made love, had he ever known the wonder and the glory of what he experienced as he kissed Florencia.

He knew as he did so that for her it was the first time she had been kissed, and because he could read her thoughts he knew that what she was feeling was part of her prayers and part, too, of the beauty with which she was surrounded and which was intrinsically a part of herself.

Only when he took his mouth from hers and she hid her face against his neck did he say softly:

'Now you know, my darling, why I will save you, and why nothing and nobody will stand in my way or prevent you from being free to marry me.'

She did not answer and he knew she was crying, but her tears were now of happiness and hope.

Lord Mere did not underestimate the danger both to himself of being discovered and the threat to Florencia's reputation so he kissed her again until he felt as if they both touched the stars and were enveloped by the light of the moon, he said:

'I must leave you, my darling, and you must go to sleep. Believe in me, remember that I need your prayers.'

'I shall pray for you without ceasing,' Florencia answered. 'At the same time, I want to thank God that he sent you to save us.'

'You must not speak about it to anybody,' Lord Mere said warningly, 'not even to your father or your brother. Do you understand?'

'I understand.'

'It must be a secret—our secret!'

She turned her face up to his and he looked down at her for a long moment.

'You have been in my heart ever since I can remember,' he said, 'but I never thought I would find you outside a painting.'

'But I am here..and I am..real.'

'I know that,' he said, 'and I swear to you, my precious darling, that I will die rather than allow you to marry any man, let alone that devil who is torturing your father!'

Florencia gave a little cry.

'Suppose he..injures you..or..kills you?'

'I will take great care of myself for your sake.'

He kissed her again; a loving tender kiss that made them both feel as if they were floating in the air, miles away from the earth.

Then as they came back to reality Lord Mere rose from the bed with a sigh.

'Goodnight, my precious, my beautiful wife-to-be!' he said.

The deepness of his voice and the love in his eyes made her lift her lips to his, but he only took her hands, one after the other, kissed then gently, and turned them over to kiss the palms passionately and insistently.

Then, as if he forced himself to do so, he walked across the room to the window.

Only as he moved between the curtains did he look back to see her watching him, her eyes wide and apprehensive, her hands clasped as if she was already praying for him.

He smiled at her, then the curtains closed behind him and he swung himself over the balcony and started slowly and painstakingly to descend to the ground.

★ ★ ★ ★

Hicks was waiting where Lord Mere had left him and they rode away, at first quietly through the woods in case anybody should hear them go.

Then when they reached the open land and the moonlight was bright enough for them to see their way without worrying they galloped as hard as they could back towards the Villa.

Only when they had put the horses back

in the stable and Hicks was helping Lord Mere to undress did they speak for the first time.

'Tomorrow you have to visit Prince di Gorizia's *Palazzo,*' Lord Mere said. 'I want you, Hicks, to be as clever as you have been today, and most important of all to find out in which room Prince Vincente sleeps, and the easiest way to approach it.'

'You don't want to push yer luck, M'Lord,' Hicks said.

'It is something I have to do,' Lord Mere replied, 'and you know I must rely on you, Hicks, to find out everything you can.'

It would be impossible for him to call on the Gorizias, unless...

He paused for a moment.

He thought suddenly that while it would be a mistake for Sir Julius to take him there, who had made it quite obvious what he thought of the Gorizias, it would be a very different thing if he were taken by the *Contessa.*

By the time Hicks had left him he was in bed, but he was not sleeping.

His brain was working with a swift intensity that in the past had made him so successful on many different missions he had undertaken in Europe.

He had learned never to underestimate the possible value of a contact made with anyone, however insignificant or unimportant they might seem to be in his general scheme.

Somebody in the past, and he could not remember now who it was, had said: 'Even the smallest pebble can make a large ripple,' and it was something he had always remembered.

He felt now that while he had imagined the *Contessa* was unimportant to him since he had met Florencia, she quite definitely could have her uses.

When finally he shut his eyes and prepared himself for sleep, a plan was already laid out in his mind in which every move was calculated.

At the same time, although his confederates in past episodes might not believe it, he was taking as few chances as possible not for his own sake, but for Florencia's.

★ ★ ★ ★

When Lord Mere came down to breakfast
he was served on the verandah outside the
Dining-Room, but there was no sign of
his host.

Even when he had slept for only three
or four hours, he felt fresh and alert, and
not in the least tired.

He had trained himself over the years to
get by with as much or as little sleep as
was necessary without feeling the loss of
it when he was obliged to work late hours
during the night.

He was not surprised when as soon as he
had seated himself at the breakfast table a
servant came to say:

'I regret to inform you, M'Lord, that
sir Julius has had a restless night and
has therefore decided to stay in bed until
lunchtime.'

'I quite understand,' Lord Mere answered.
'Tell Sir Julius I think he is wise, and as I
have a call to make in the City, I know he
will understand if I borrow his carriage.'

★ ★ ★ ★

Later in the morning Lord Mere drove to the house of the *Contessa* Mazara stopping only on the way to purchase a large basket of orchids which he thought were an appropriate flower for the lady in question.

In the shop there were also some very lovely lilies that reminded him of Florencia.

He longed to send them to her, but knew to do so would be a mistake.

He thought however that the day would come when he would surround her with the white flowers that matched her purity and which were somehow always associated in his mind with Raphael's pictures of the Madonna.

It took a short time for the basket of orchids to be carried out of the shop and put into the carriage. Then he drove on, deliberately putting Florencia out of his mind, in order to concentrate on the *Contessa*.

As he had anticipated, she was delighted

to see him and with little delay she swept into the room into which he had been shown.

She was wearing a most alluring garment which he was well aware was unconventional so early in the day.

'I have been so looking forward to seeing you again, My Lord,' the *Contessa* said as he kissed her hand.

'I would have called on you yesterday had it been possible,' Lord Mere replied, 'but Sir Julius took me to visit the Sogino *Palazzo.*'

The *Contessa* smiled.

'I thought he would do that, and I am sure you enjoyed the pictures.'

'They were magnificent!'

'After that, I know I shall be embarrassed to show you my own small collection,' the *Contessa* said somewhat demurely.

'You know I am looking forward to seeing it,' Lord Mere answered gallantly.

He paused, then went on:

'I am also rather curious to see the collection belonging to the Gorizias.'

'They are nothing like as good as the

145

Sogino's!' the *Contessa* said.

'I have heard that,' Lord Mere replied, 'but the Earl of Rosebery, who, as you may know, is our Foreign Secretary, was telling me they have two outstanding pictures which I should certainly try to see while I am in Florence.'

This was a bold venture, but the *Contessa* quickly supplied the answer.

'You mean the Leonardo da Vinci and the Ingres. Yes, I suppose we must concede that they are outstanding!'

'I would love to see them with you,' Lord Mere said.

He spoke in a way that was so flattering that the *Contessa* fell all too easily into the snare he had set for her and said:

'We will go together after luncheon.'

'I can imagine nothing more delightful,' Lord Mere replied.

He prevented the *Contessa* from taking him immediately to her own Picture Gallery, which he was quite certain would end in her private apartments, by saying that he had an appointment at the British Embassy.

Lord Mere promised he would return to her as quickly as possible and left her making arrangements for the afternoon, and sending a groom to inform the Prince that they would be calling on him at about a half-after-two.

Lord Mere, because he knew it was a mistake for him to tell unnecessary lies, went immediately to the British Embassy to pay his respects to the Ambassador without wasting very much time about it.

On his way back to the Villa, he stopped the carriage at the Ponte Vecchio, renowned for its Jewellers' shops, the most famous of whom was Giovanni.

Lord Mere remembered the old man from a previous visit and having shaken him by the hand sat down in his small private office.

'Can I do anything for you, My Lord?' the Jeweller asked.

Lord Mere explained that he was looking for a present for his sister and inspected some exquisite pieces of coral set with diamonds.

Finally, after some deliberation, he chose

a pair of ear-rings and a ring to match.

He also ordered a necklace to be made, together with them, and knew that they would make a special present for Florencia when he was able to give her some of the many things he planned for her.

Only when Giovanni was making out the account and one of his assistants was packing up the ear-rings and the ring did Lord Mere say casually:

'I hear you are making some repairs to the famous necklace belonging to the Soginos. I have often thought it the most fabulous piece of jewellery in the whole of Europe.'

'You are right, My Lord,' Giovanni said. 'In fact, it is a joy for me just to look at it, let alone work on it!'

He gave a little sigh. Then he said:

'I expect Prince Antonio told you that he brought it to me last night. He did not know how glad I was to see it!'

'Why particularly?' Lord Mere asked.

'Because, My Lord, there have been rumours going about Florence that the necklace had left the City. As you know, Florence is very jealous of her treasures and collectors have already been making enquiries following some malicious rumours that the Prince di Sogino was selling pictures from the *Palazzo*. Of course, I did not believe it, but you know how these things get talked about and exaggerated.'

'Of course,' Lord Mere said. 'People will make a scandal about nothing.'

'Well, I can say to anybody who asks me that the necklace is here and as beautiful as ever it was!'

'I hope you will tell everybody the truth,' Lord Mere said. 'I have a great respect for the Prince di Sogino, and I would not like to think that he was being defamed.'

'You are right, My Lord,' Giovanni said. 'He is a noble man, but like all great nobles, he has his enemies.'

There was no doubt of whom he was speaking, and Lord Mere said with a feigned air of surprise:

'Surely those old-fashioned, ridiculous vendettas of the last century are not continued today?'

'I am afraid they are,' Giovanni said,

'and there is a rumour although I cannot believe it is true, that Princess Florencia di Sogino is to marry Prince Vincente di Gorizia.'

Lord Mere looked surprised.

'I can hardly believe that is true! From all I hear, he is not a particularly desirable young man.'

'He is wicked, My Lord! Really wicked! If you knew of the way he is behaving almost every night in the low part of the City, you would be appalled!'

The old Jeweller spoke with a note of disgust in his voice which told Lord Mere that what Sir Julius had said to him of Prince Vincente's excesses was undoubtedly true.

'Is there nothing that can be done to prevent him from behaving in such a manner?' he asked. 'Surely his victims, and their parents, must hate him!'

'They would kill him, My Lord, if they got the chance,' Giovanni said.

His voice dropped as he added:

'I believe one man who was incensed by the Prince's behaviour towards his daughter attacked him, but the Prince's body-guard—he always has one with him at night—killed him first!'

'A pity!' Lord Mere remarked laconically.

He rose to his feet as he spoke, having found out what he wanted to know.

His package was ready for him, and he said goodbye to Giovanni.

Walking back to his carriage he drove back to the Villa knowing that after luncheon the *Contessa* would be eagerly awaiting him with an invitation in her dark eyes that would be even more insistent than it had been on the night he had met her.

5

Driving in the *Contessa*'s open carriage towards the Gorizia *Palazzo* Lord Mere had to admit that she was an extremely attractive woman.

He knew that if he had not fallen in love

precipitately and seriously with Florencia, he would certainly have amused himself with her while he was in Florence.

Sophisticated, worldly-wise, and with a sharp wit usually at somebody else's expense, the *Contessa* was exceedingly good company, and at the same time made it very clear how attractive she found him.

They talked of many things as they drove through the sunlit City, but he was well aware there was an innuendo behind most of her words, and an expression in her eyes that told him far more than what she said with her lips.

When he saw the Gorizia *Palazzo* it was coarser in structure and without the elegance which seemed very much part of the Sogino family.

There was too, he realised, a high wall encircling the garden which he did not look forward to scaling at night.

However Lord Mere never accepted defeat, and his brain was working like a well-oiled machine, noticing and memorising every detail of the structure of the house as they were shown from the Main

Hall up a staircase to the Reception Room on the First Floor.

The Prince di Gorizia was waiting for them, and as he greeted them Lord Mere thought again how ugly he looked and that he had none of the aristocratic distinction of his enemy.

The Prince however was very effusive.

'It is an inestimable pleasure to see you, *Contessa*,' he said as he kissed her hand, 'and I am of course flattered that the reputable Lord Mere should wish to visit my *Palazzo!*'

'He has heard from the Earl of Rosebery about your Leonardo da Vinci,' the *Contessa* said, 'and as he is an insatiable collector of pictures himself, he could not bear to leave Forence without seeing it.'

'Of course not!' the Prince agreed. 'But first I want you to taste some wine from my own vineyards which I flatter myself is superior to any I have produced before!'

It was certainly Lord Mere thought, a pleasantly light and appetising wine, and he noticed that the Prince took several glasses.

'When I received your note,' he was saying to the *Contessa,* 'I was just about to write to you to ask you to dine with me tonight because unexpectedly several of my cousins have arrived here from Rome, and as they are young, I want to give a party for them and emulate the delightful evening I spent with you the night before last.'

The *Contessa's* face fell.

'Oh, Your Highness, it is too disappointing!' she exclaimed, 'but I have a party of my own, not a large one, but as it includes several very old friends, I could not throw them over at the last moment.'

'A disappointment indeed!' the Prince said. 'But I hope, Lord Mere, that you will accept the invitation to dine with me, and of course I should be delighted to see Sir Julius.'

'I am afraid Sir Julius is indisposed,' Lord Mere replied, 'but I would be only too pleased to accept your invitation rather than dine alone at the Villa.'

He spoke quickly, knowing perceptively that the *Contessa* was about to invite him to dine with her, and he had the idea it was what she had been planning all along.

But as he was very anxious to see as much of the inside of the Gorizia *Palazzo* as he could, the invitation could not have been more opportune.

'Then that is settled,' the Prince said. 'If you could be here at about eight o'clock, I feel that you will enjoy meeting my cousins, all of whom are extremely attractive.'

Lord Mere saw the expression in the *Contessa*'s eyes, and afraid that she might in some way upset the arrangement he said:

'You are very kind, but as Sir Julius is unfortunately indisposed, you will understand that I will not wish to stay late.'

He knew as he spoke that the *Contessa* drew in her breath, assuming that he really intended to join her later after the dinner.

The Prince put down his glass.

'And now,' he said, 'you must come and admire my Leonardo da Vinci, but I hope that some of my other paintings will please you too, which despite the competition I have to endure from the Soginos, are considered very fine.'

Lord Mere had to concede that this was true when he saw a very fine Vasari and, although he had not expected it, a Raphael entitled: *'Lady with a Veil'*.

It did not resemble Florencia.

At the same time because it was by his favourite artist he stood in front of it for a long time before the Prince persuaded him to move on and look at the Leonardo da Vinci, which was indeed everything he had hoped.

There were other fine pictures, and in any other City except Florence Lord Mere knew they would have been acclaimed and extolled by every visitor who was privileged to see them.

He could understand in a way how it gave the Prince a great deal of pleasure to know that his son's blackmail of the Soginos had forced them to sell part of their collection which had existed longer than his and was larger and finer.

Having looked at the pictures Lord Mere

now looked out through the windows of the Gallery, building up in his mind a plan of the whole building.

There was a good excuse for doing so, for the view outside was a fine one, although not, he thought, quite as magnificent as that from the Sogino *Palazzo*.

The whole building was however considerably larger and as they turned to walk back to the Reception Room he said: 'I cannot help feeling, Your Highness, that you will feel very lonely here when your son leaves you after he is married.'

'Leaves me?' the Prince echoed. 'He will certainly not do that! Vincente has the whole of the West Wing to himself and I can assure you there is plenty of room there for a wife and a dozen children!'

The way he spoke gave Lord Mere a feeling of revulsion at the idea of anything so exquisite and innocent as Florencia bearing the children of a lecher like Vincente.

But he had found out what he wished to know, and as if she was aware that it interested him the *Contessa* said:

'You must show Lord Mere the beautiful garden below the West Wing, Your Highness. It is something of which I am deeply envious, especially the fountain, which is quite one of the most beautiful I have ever seen!'

'Of course he can see it,' the Prince agreed.

He was obviously enjoying showing off his possessions and boasting about them.

It was almost as if he challenged his distinguished guest to find fault with or not to admire the Gorizias.

They went down the stairs to what Lord Mere now knew was the foot of the West Tower, where there was a garden that he immediately agreed was one of the most beautiful he had ever seen.

It was small, encircled by a white marble wall, and the centre-piece was a fountain erected on six steps which had been sculpted by Ammanati.

He looked at it, noting the beautifully portrayed cupids at the foot of the bowl, and the sculpture rising high about it.

He then realised that at the top there

were two figures depicting *'The Rape of Proserpina'*.

For a moment, as he remembered to whom the garden belonged, everything seemed to swim in front of his eyes.

Then in a voice that did not sound like his own, he heard himself say:

'A very fine sculpture! No wonder you are proud of it!'

'Very proud,' the Prince replied, 'and you must agree it is his best work.'

Because he could not bear to look at the figure of Proserpina struggling against her captor, Lord Mere turned his back on it and examined some of the other sculptures on the other side of the small garden.

It was obvious that the *Contessa* was anxious to leave and have him on her own, and although it took a little time, they gradually wended their way back to the Reception Room.

But not before Lord Mere had a good look at the West Tower.

He thought he knew, although he could not be sure, where the most important rooms were, and jutting out from the tower inside the garden itself was a crenellated rampart where in times past defenders must have waited for their approaching enemies.

The battlements on the top of the *Palazzo* were the same, and he thought how much simpler it would be if today, instead of scheming how he could rescue Florencia, he could declare war against her enemies.

However, he was far too diplomatic and self-controlled not to be able to say goodbye to the Prince with what sounded a sincere appreciation of his hospitality.

Then he assured him that he was greatly looking forward to dining with him that evening.

'It will not be such a large party as our dear friend the *Contessa* had the other evening,' the Prince said, 'but we shall be about twenty for dinner and I am sure Vincente will ask some of his young friends to come in afterwards and dance.'

'It sounds most enjoyable,' Lord Mere replied, following the *Contessa* who had already stepped into her carriage.

They drove off and as soon as they were out of earshot the *Contessa* cried:

'I could not be more mortified! If I had known you were alone this evening, I would have invited you to dine with me.'

She paused before she added:

'For you, My Lord, I would certainly have put off my friends.'

'How can I have been so foolish as not to mention it?' Lord Mere asked. 'I ought to have told you that Sir Julius was indisposed, but if I leave the Prince early perhaps your party will not yet have come to an end.'

That, he knew, was what the *Contessa* was expecting him to say.

She put her hand through his arm as she replied:

'I shall be hoping the lovely ladies from Rome will not prevent you from coming to me.'

She was far too experienced in the ways of enticing a man to say any more, or to emphasise how much she wanted him.

She merely contrived to make him laugh, and as she drove him back to Sir Julius's

Villa they talked of everything except what would happen later in the evening.

Only when, as the horses drew up outside Sir Julius's front door and Lord Mere alighted and kissed the *Contessa*'s hand in farewell, did she say:

'My party, and it will be quite a large one, will certainly not break up until dawn!'

Lord Mere did not reply. He merely smiled and as the *Contessa* drove off he knew that she was not disappointed with the time they has spent together.

Inside the Villa he learned that Sir Julius was sleeping, and going into one of the cool quiet rooms he sat down at a desk and started to draw a plan of the Gorizia *Palazzo*.

He knew that luck was on his side in that he had been invited to dinner and would not have to face what would have been a very hazardous task of entering the building by stealth.

He thought that the high wall completely enclosed the Prince's garden, and he had noticed that the gates were opened for

162

them when they arrived and closed when they left.

The walls on the outside of the *Palazzo*, although more roughly constructed, had not the footholds there had been for his climb of the previous evening.

There was also no balcony leading into what he imagined was Prince Vincente's private rooms.

To be inside the *Palazzo* as a guest would certainly make things easier—or perhaps more difficult—he was not sure.

He could only trust in his fate and his instinct which so far had never failed him.

And when he thought of Ammanati's 'Rape of Proserpina' and of Florencia he told himself that he must save her, even if he died in the attempt.

Everything he had been told about Prince Vincente seemed to haunt his mind for the rest of the evening.

He thought of the excesses to which he knew no decent man would stoop, and how, for all he had heard, the Prince revelled in the filth of the gutter, and was vicious to the point of sadism.

The more he thought of it, the more it seemed to him unspeakable that the Soginos could agree to the match between Florencia and Vincente di Gorizia.

At the same time he could understand that for Prince di Sogino to be accused of disloyalty to the King, to be treated as a common criminal and perhaps shot, would be a disgrace and humiliation to everybody who bore his name.

'I must save her! I must save her!' Lord Mere told himself.

Because his heart as well as his mind cried out that it was imperative, he felt for the first time in his life not entirely confident that he would succeed.

He rose from the desk at which he had been sitting and moving across the room went out through a French window into the garden.

He stood looking down at the panorama of Florence beneath him and he thought how much beauty its painters, its sculptors and its craftsmen had contributed to the world.

But there had also been cruelty and treachery, and that too had left its mark on its people, so that history lived again in them, in their emotions, their aspirations and their ambitions.

He found himself thinking of Florencia's beauty and knew it was also part of the beauty of all the Madonnas that Raphael had painted.

Because it was a beauty and a purity that was in itself Divine, Lord Mere knew he was not alone in his crusade to save her.

He was aware of a Power greater than himself and ready to help him, whom he now called upon for the first time since he had left School.

His prayer, as he uttered it, came from the very depths of his soul.

★ ★ ★ ★

Looking round the Banqueting Hall where the Prince's dinner was taking place, Lord Mere thought it was difficult to detach himself from what appeared to be an ordinary though luxurious dinner-party given in an aristocrat's house.

The silver ornaments on the table were magnificent; the candles with which the room was lit shone on the glittering jewels of the Prince's guests and made even him seem to have a distinction that was missing in the daytime.

The food was excellent, the wine, which the Prince boasted came from his own vineyards, certainly very palatable.

There was a footman behind every chair, wearing an elaborate, almost medieval livery of claret and purple, gorgeously ornamented with a profusion of gold braid.

It was only when he looked at Prince Vincente that Lord Mere knew that the young man seemed to be even more loathsome than he had appeared to be the first night he had met him.

When he touched his hand in greeting he felt as though he was a reptile, a venomous cobra from which any man would shrink in horror.

The Prince was however being extremely effusive to one of his very attractive cousins who, as his father had, had just arrived from Rome.

She was however more experienced than she appeared and was parrying his flattery with an expertise which might have been admired in an older woman.

On the other side of the Prince was another cousin, a young girl of about fifteen years of age who was obviously thrilled at attending what was probably her first large dinner-party.

She was looking round her with curious eyes and was a pretty child with long hair nearly to her waist. She might, Lord Mere thought, have sat as a model for one of Botticelli's spring-like figures.

He had on one side of him an extremely charming Florentine who had spent a great deal of time in Paris, and on the other one of their hosts' cousins who had arrived from Rome.

The conversation was witty and amusing, and he knew if he had not been concentrating on something far more important and fundamental, he would have enjoyed the evening.

When dinner came to an end they all moved to a delightful room on the Ground Floor with windows which opened onto a terrace and where already an Orchestra was playing softly.

The room was fashioned rather in the style of a Roman Hall with pillars, statues and a well-painted mural at one end of it.

Because Lord Mere had no desire to dance, he studied the mural, then found the Lady from Rome who had sat next to him at dinner and suggested that they look at some of the pictures in the other rooms.

'I would love to do that,' she said. 'Although I am a relative this is my first visit to the *Palazzo* and I have not yet had an opportunity of seeing all the beautiful things it contains.

'Then let me be your guide,' Lord Mere replied, 'although a rather inadequate one, as I only came here for the first time today myself!'

She laughed.

'I heard that you visited the Soginos

yesterday. You are certainly an ardent sight-seer!'

'I prefer to be thought of as an appreciator of beauty!' Lord Mere answered.

He managed to make the words a compliment and she looked at him coyly.

Then just as they were moving up the stairs to the next floor somebody from behind them called out:

'Marsalla! My father insists that we start the dancing, and you promised you would dance with me!'

'But, of course!' Marsalla replied. 'Forgive me, My Lord, and let me join you as soon as I am free.'

'I shall be waiting,' Lord Mere promised.

Marsalla ran down the stairs to where Vincente was waiting, and Lord Mere realised this was his opportunity.

He was standing half-hidden by an arrangement of flowers and he thought the Prince had not seen with whom Marsalla was talking.

Taking a chance, he hurried up the staircase and remembering the rough plan he had drawn of the layout of the *Palazzo*, found his way without much difficulty to the West Tower.

He did not forget however Giovanni's warning that Prince Vincente had a body-guard, which was why he had deliberately brought Hicks with him this evening in the front of the carriage.

He had told him to introduce himself to the other household servants and, if it was possible, to keep the Prince's body-guard out of the way.

Because he knew what was expected of him, Hicks had risen to the occasion.

'I think it'd be a good idea, M'Lord,' he said as he helped Lord Mere to dress, 'if I takes with me that flask you carries in your pocket when Your Lordship goes out shooting.'

'Yes, of course,' Lord Mere had agreed.

'You can drink half a dozen bottles of their wine,' Hicks went on, 'without it going to yer head, but brandy's a different kettle o'fish!'

'I will leave it to you to do what you think is best,' Lord Mere said.

'Be careful, M'Lord,' Hicks warned.

'They're nasty customers, that lot, from all I 'ears! An' that's an understatement!'

Lord Mere was certain Hicks was right.

Moving quickly, he found first the Prince's bedroom, then saw that next to it was a large and impressive Sitting-Room.

He knew, now that the banquet had finished, it was likely that the Prince's valet and the rest of his servants would be enjoying a meal in the kitchen quarters.

Therefore it was unlikely he would have a better opportunity than now of finding the safe.

Florencia had told him that the safe was in Vincente's bedroom, and he thought, although he was not sure, that it would be disguised in some way, and there was certainly no sign of it at first glance.

He opened first a beautifully inlaid chest that must have been made by some craftsman in the 16th century.

There was a gold key that turned in a gold lock, and as the door opened he saw not a safe but a collection of whips and chains and other instruments of eroticism.

171

It made him press his lips together in a hard line and he shut the door again quickly.

The mere thought of Florencia coming in contact with a man who kept such things in his bedroom made him feel physically sick.

Then he forced himself not to think of Florencia but of the urgency of his search.

It took him only a few minutes to find the safe was in a far corner of the room, disguised as a table.

It was quite a clever idea to put a round piece of wood over it, and cover it over with a heavy velvet cloth deeply fringed which made it seem very much part of the other decorations in the room.

The safe was a new one, but Lord Mere had taken a secret course in London in learning how to open any safe that was yet available on the market.

This happened to be one of a make very like one he owned himself, and it took him only two or three minutes to work out the combination and open it.

Inside the safe there were a number of shelves and on the top one there were velvet boxes which he guessed contained jewels.

On the second there were documents, and he had the idea that if he had time they would be very revealing and doubtless incriminating to their owner.

But he was at the moment only concerned with saving Florencia's father, and on the bottom shelf he discovered what he was looking for.

Because he owned one of the new Facile cameras himself, it was not difficult to find the roll of film.

He was greatly relieved that the negatives were on film which had not long been introduced, for he had feared they might be on glass plates which would be far more difficult for him to conceal about his person.

There were three rolls of film which was rather surprising, and he wondered if they were all of the Prince di Sogino until he found some prints on the same shelf.

A quick glance told him they were the

ones he was seeking, but there were also others which he suspected might be used for blackmailing other people in the same way that Vincente was blackmailing the Prince.

He slipped them all quickly into the tails of his evening-coat.

Then having cleared the shelf he was just about to close the door of the safe when he saw on the bottom of it something he recognised.

Last month he had had occasion to visit Scotland Yard, and the Commissioner had shown him a quantity of drugs they had recently taken from a man who had brought them illegally into England.

The drugs on the bottom of the safe looked exactly similar, and Lord Mere was aware this was another reason why Prince Vincente needed so much money.

He glanced at them, then quickly closed the safe, setting it on the same combination and pulling down the elaborate velvet cloth which made it once again appear nothing more significant than a round table.

Moving silently across the room, he

paused at the door.

He knew it was vital that nobody should see him leaving the Prince's apartments, and to his relief there was nobody about.

He shut the door of the Prince's bedroom behind him and started to walk swiftly along the passage.

As he did so, he heard a very different sound.

He paused, then realised that what he had heard was a woman screaming.

He told himself it was vitally important for him to get away from the West Tower immediately.

Then the screams came again.

Now he cautiously looked out from a window and saw that just below him there was the rampart he had noticed from the garden when he had been shown the fountain by Ammanati.

It was nearly dark, but he could see a white gown and a woman struggling violently against a man.

"It is none of my business!" Lord Mere thought quickly.

Then as he would have turned away

towards the stairs, he saw a strand of long unbound hair fly out of her struggle and realised it was the young girl of fifteen who had sat next to Prince Vincente at dinner.

As he recognised her, he saw at the same time that the man who was struggling with her was the Prince.

He was dragging her towards a couch which was arranged with several garden chairs on the rampart.

Lord Mere looking through the open window heard her cry:

'No..no! Leave me..alone!'

The Prince did not answer, and from the way he was trying to push her onto the couch Lord Mere knew in horror what he was intending to do.

Inflamed through drugs, or excited by a lust which made him seek out very young girls who were little more than children, Prince Vincente intended to repeat the story of the statue which stood in the garden below him.

Suddenly, whatever the risk to himself, Lord Mere knew he could not allow this to happen.

He had not even spoke to the girl, but that she was very young, innocent, and untouched had been obvious as he sat opposite her at dinner.

For a moment she became identified in his mind with Florencia.

He ran down the stairs and instead of continuing along the corridor the way he had come, he took a few steps further down the side of the tower to where he found a door leading onto the rampart.

It was open, and by the time Lord Mere reached it, Prince Vincente had thrown the young girl down on the couch and had flung himself on top of her.

She was screaming but completely helpless, and as Lord Mere neared them he could hear her pleading piteously:

'No, no! Please..do not do this! Oh, God..save...me!'

She gave a shriek of horror as the Prince tore her gown from her breast, and as he did so Lord Mere seized him by the back of his coat and dragged him off the couch and onto his feet.

'Stop that, you swine!' he exclaimed.

'What the devil do you think you are doing?' the Prince ejaculated. 'This is none of your business!'

'I beg to differ,' Lord Mere replied. 'You will stop violating that young girl, or I will make you sorry you were ever born.'

He spoke with a violence that was unusual when he was involved in a confrontation of this sort.

But the thought that the Prince might have been raping Florencia made him forget everything but his hatred of anything so cruel and bestial.

Then as the Prince eyed him furiously and the two men faced each other, the girl realising she had been saved jumped to her feet and ran sobbing hysterically back into the *Palazzo*.

With an almost superhuman effort, Lord Mere forced himself to say:

'You must forgive my interference, Your Highness, but really that child was too young for such grown-up games!'

'You meddlesome, interfering Englishman!' the Prince snarled. 'I will kill you for this!'

As he spoke his hand went into the inside pocket of his coat, and as he drew out something that glinted evilly in his hand Lord Mere realised suddenly the danger he was in.

The pupils of the Prince's eyes were noticeably enlarged, which indicated that he was under the influence of drugs, and he had also drunk a great deal at dinner.

Lord Mere was well aware that he would kill him without the slightest compunction.

As the Prince steadied himself, the stiletto poised in his hand ready to strike, Lord Mere felt suddenly cool and calm, as he always did in moments of acute danger.

He also knew irrefutably that the Power he had called on earlier in the day was with him, protecting him, guiding him.

He knew then that the only possible way to save himself was to act first.

With the swiftness and poise of an athlete whose body synchronised perfectly with his mind, he moved before the Prince could raise his arm to strike and hit him on the point of the chin.

He used every ounce of strength in his body, and it was strictly according to the Queensberry Rules.

As the Prince staggered and the stiletto dropped from his hand and clattered to the ground, Lord Mere hit him again, this time lifting him off his feet so that he fell backwards, onto the crenellated battlements where the lower wall of an embrasure caught him behind his knees, and incapable of saving himself, he fell back off the rampart and disappeared from view.

For a moment Lord Mere could hardly believe what had happened.

Then as he stepped forward to look down, he saw directly in line with the Ammanati fountain the Prince's body lying sprawled.

It was a drop of some forty feet and it was obviously that he had broken his neck.

Lord Mere stood for a moment looking down at the still body, a dark patch on the white stone. Then he turned and walked quickly away.

He climbed the few stairs up to the main corridor, then descended the other staircase by which he had reached the West Tower.

It took him only seconds to find his way to the Picture Gallery which he had intended to inspect with Marsalla.

As he reached it he saw her coming towards him, her pretty pink and silver gown shining in the light of the gas-globes which lit this part of the *Palazzo*.

He walked swiftly towards her and she exclaimed:

'Oh, there you are! I have come back to you as I promised, but I was afraid you would not want...'

'I have been looking for the best pictures to show you,' he answered, 'and now we can look at them together and not waste our time on the ones that are less important.'

He spoke quite easily and calmly although his heart was still thumping from the experience through which he had just passed.

'I am sorry I went away in that rude

181

manner,' she said confidingly, 'and I did not enjoy my dance. Vincente had had too much to drink at dinner, so I made the excuse that I wanted to speak to my mother and left him as quickly as I could.'

'You were quite right,' Lord Mere said. 'Dancing with a man who has had too much to drink must be a very unpleasant experience.'

She laughed.

'I am afraid my Cousin Vincente is a very naughty boy! But do not let us talk about him. Show me the pictures you have found for me.'

'There are two or three delightful ones which you might have sat for yourself,' Lord Mere said.

Because he knew she expected it, he kissed her lightly at the end of the Gallery, then took her back to the Ball-Room saying:

'It would be a mistake to ruin your reputation on the first night you arrive in Florence.'

'Shall I see you again while you are here?' she asked.

'I promise I will make every effort,' he answered, 'but I feel you will have so many invitations that you will not have time for me.'

'Oh, but I will!' she objected.

He handed her back to her relations and while she was being teased for having left the Ball-Room he slipped away.

He had not intended to leave the party so soon, but then he had a sudden idea.

Once Vincente's body had been found, which might not be for an hour or so, perhaps longer, it was important that he should have an alibi.

Although he had suggested that he should visit the *Contessa* later, he had not really meant to do so. However he had deliberately left the invitation open, having a strange feeling that it might come in useful.

Now he knew that once again fate was on his side and he was being helped in an almost magical manner.

It would be impossible for anybody to implicate him in any way in Vincente's death if it was believed that he had gone from the Prince's party early to visit the *Contessa* and had spent at least half the night there.

The young girl might tell her mother of her terrible experience with Vincente and that she had been rescued but he was aware that most young girls would be too shy and embarrassed to relate what had happened.

Even if she did say that she had been rescued at the last moment from what she and her family would consider a 'fate worse than death', he was sure she had been in too hysterical a condition to be able to recognise her rescuer in the dark.

'What I have to do is to make certain that everybody concerned knows where I am for the next few hours,' Lord Mere told himself.

He went up to two or three of the guests to bid them goodbye before he approached his host.

'Leaving so early?' one of them asked.

'I promised the *Contessa* Mazara that I would drop in at the party she is giving tonight,' Lord Mere explained. 'It is always the same—two delightful invitations on one evening, and then days of boredom with nothing to look forward to!'

The man laughed.

'That is only too true,' he said, 'and I know how amusing the *Contessa*'s parties always are!'

Lord Mere said much the same thing to his host who was very sympathetic.

'I thought the *Contessa* was rather annoyed that I got my invitation in first,' he said. 'You should not be so popular, young man! But I understand that you "want to have your cake and eat it!"'

He laughed at his own joke and was very pleased that he had managed to say the last words in English.

Lord Mere laughed too.

'I must tell the *Contessa* what you have said,' he replied, 'and thank you for a delightful dinner. I have enjoyed myself enormously.'

The Prince was polite enough to take him to the front door, and when Lord Mere had driven away he sat back for a moment against the soft cushions of the carriage and closed his eyes.

He could hardly believe he had been so successful.

And yet everything throughout the whole evening seemed to have gone almost to the rhythm of music.

The music of a Funeral March, but also the music of Victory.

6

Lord Mere let the carriage drive in the direction of the City for a little while before he knocked on the communicating window.

The coachman brought the horses to a standstill and when the footman opened the door to see what he required he said:

'I wish to visit the *Contessa* Mazara but as I see my man is with you, we will set him down at the gate of the Villa as we pass by it. But first, as I have something to say to him, tell him to join me inside.'

The footman immediately called Hicks down from the box and he stepped into the carriage to sit with his back to the horses.

As they drove on Lord Mere said:

'Thank you, Hicks. You obviously managed to keep the Prince's body-guard under control.'

'It wasn't easy, M'Lord,' Hicks replied. 'He were a restless sort of chap, but after he'd drunk half the contents of Your Lordship's flask I slipped into it one of them white pills we've used before.'

Lord Mere raised his eye-brows, but did not speak and Hicks went on:

'Passed out like a light, he did! A few minutes later the whole staff were jeering at him for getting dead drunk!'

Lord Mere felt a sense of relief.

He had reckoned that the first person to find the dead body of the Prince would almost certainly be his body-guard and he knew now that the knock-out pill Hicks had given him would keep him insensible for at least five hours.

He thought to himself that fortune had never smiled on him so kindly as it was doing tonight, and he was sure it was due to Florencia's prayers.

Then realising that Hicks was waiting expectantly for his instructions, he said:

'Now what I want you to do, Hicks, is rather difficult, but I am sure you will do it, as you always do, exactly as I wish you to.'

'I'll do me best, M'Lord,' Hicks answered.

Five minutes later the carriage arrived at the gate of Sir Julius's Villa which stood high above them silhouetted against the sky.

Hicks jumped out of the carriage and said respectfully:

'Goodnight, M'Lord,' then waited until the carriage moved on.

It was not yet midnight when Lord Mere arrived at the *Contessa*'s mansion.

The linkmen were outside with their flares and the row of waiting carriages told Lord Mere that nobody yet was thinking of leaving the party.

When he arrived and was announced the *Contessa* gave a cry of delight at seeing him.

She moved towards him with a serpentine grace, shimmering with diamonds which were no brighter than the light in her eyes.

'You have come!' she said. 'You kept your promise! I was afraid I would be disappointed!'

'How could I disappoint you?' Lord Mere asked, kissing her hand.

He was introduced to the older members of the party, while the younger ones were dancing to the same Orchestra that had played the previous night.

He had been right in thinking that the party was not a large one, but he could see that the guests sitting near the *Contessa* were obviously close friends and undoubtedly curious about him.

They eyed him speculatively and asked discreet but searching questions concerning his reasons for being in Florence and whether he had enjoyed the party at the Gorizia *Palazzo*.

'I think the people of Florence must have a predilection for parties of this sort,' Lord Mere replied lightly, 'which are a much more pleasant form of entertaining than the huge, pompous Balls people give in London at the moment.'

He saw that his listeners were gratified by the compliment and they asked him about the Queen and other members of the Royal Family.

He was sure from the way they spoke that the *Contessa* had made him out to be even more important than he was.

He thought however it fitted in well with his plans and he answered good-humouredly every question that was put to him, at the same time making it quite obvious that his interest lay in his hostess.

He persuaded her to dance with him, and as they moved around the floor she said:

'I hope you are not in a hurry to return to the Villa. My friends will not stay late, and then it would be delightful to be able to talk to you—alone.'

It was quite obvious what she meant by

'alone' and Lord Mere replied:

'That is what I was hoping you would say, and it is needless to add that I shall be counting the minutes until your very charming, but unnecessary friends depart.'

He felt her move a little closer to him, and once again he thought that if he were not in love with Florencia he and the *Contessa* might have had a very amusing time together.

Although it seemed incredible, from the first moment he had seen Florencia's face and known it was she who haunted him from Raphael's pictures ever since he was old enough to appreciate them, it was impossible for him to find any other woman alluring.

But the *Contessa* was a vital part of his plan, and he was aware that her friends were not missing the little intimate glances between them, and her obvious delight at his arrival.

When the dance ended and they went back to the sofa on which they had previously been sitting, there was that sudden silence from the other people grouped around them that indicated to Lord Mere clearly that they had been talking about him and the *Contessa*.

At last as if they realised they were *de trop* the more elderly of the *Contessa*'s friends rose to their feet saying:

'I think we should be leaving, my dear.'

The *Contessa* did not press them to stay.

She merely said how delightful it had been to be able to entertain them, and hoped they would meet again tomorrow at the luncheon that was being given by some mutual friends.

That they were leaving was a signal for the rest of the party also to begin to make their departure. They were moving towards the door when a footman came in to say to Lord Mere in a voice that was quite audible to everybody else:

'Your servant's here, M'Lord. He informs me that he must speak to you immediately, and it's very urgent!'

Lord Mere looked surprised.

'I cannot imagine what he wants,' he remarked.

Then he looked at the *Contessa* and asked:

'You do not think that Sir Julius is ill?'

The *Contessa* clasped her hands together.

'Oh, my God! I hope it is not that!' she exclaimed.

'Send my man to me here immediately!' Lord Mere said to the flunkey.

'Is Sir Julius really ill?' somebody asked.

'I saw him for a moment before I left for dinner,' Lord Mere replied. 'He admitted to feeling somewhat fatigued, but he did not consider it serious enough to send for the doctor.'

As he finished speaking Hicks came hurrying into the room.

He had smartened himself up since returning from the Gorizia *Palazzo* and looked the part of a perfect English man-servant.

'Excuse me, M'Lord,' he said as he bowed, 'but have to inform you that a Queen's Messenger has arrived at the Villa. He says it's extremely important he should see Your Lordship with the least possible delay.'

193

'A Queen's Messenger!' Lord Mere exclaimed in astonishment. 'Did he give you any idea what he wants?'

'He did say, M'Lord, that he'd been instructed by Her Majesty to ask you to return to England immediately!'

'Did he give any reason?'

'I understands, M'Lord, somebody of great importance be visiting Her Majesty at Windsor Castle, and Her Majesty requires you to entertain her guest during his stay.'

Hicks was speaking in English, but Lord Mere was well aware that almost everybody in the room spoke English and not only understood what was being said, but was also listening attentively to every word.

'Thank you Hicks,' he said. 'I presume the carriage is outside?'

'Yes, M'Lord. Two as it happens. I comes here on the Queen's Messenger's instructions as quickly as I could!'

'Quite right!' Lord Mere approved.

Hicks bowed respectfully and turned away towards the door and Lord Mere made a gesture with his hands that was very eloquent.

'How could I have guessed, how could I have imagined,' he said to the *Contessa*, 'that Her Majesty would cut short my visit to Florence in such a drastic manner?'

'I suppose it is a Royal Command which you must obey,' the *Contessa* said wistfully.

'I have no alternative,' he replied. 'The Queen's Messenger will be waiting at the Villa, my instructions will be in writing, and I shall learn then who this important visitor is.'

He made a grimace as he added:

'He doubtless speaks some unintelligible language which Her Majesty, with her unshakable belief in my linguistic powers, will expect me to translate.

Lord Mere laughed, but he knew those listening were intrigued, and the story would be all over Florence by the morning.

Nobody made any further move to leave and he guessed they would stay and talk over with each other what they had heard and speculate about it.

After he said goodbye to them all the *Contessa* walked alone with him from the room into the passage which led into the Hall.

'Fate is against us!' she said in a low voice.

'That is exactly what I was deploring!'

'You will come back another time?'

'I have not seen or done half the things I want to do in Florence,' he answered, and knew she took the words to mean the promise of a quick return.

Because there were servants in the Hall he could only kiss her hand, forcing his lips to linger on the softness of her skin before she said goodbye with a frustrated look in her dark eyes.

Then once again Lord Mere was driving away, having extricated himself with what he thought was considerable dexterity from a very difficult situation.

He had not gone far before he stopped the carriage and told the footmen that he wished not to return to the Villa as they obviously expected but to go first to the *Palazzo* Sogino.

The servants expressed no surprise but simply turned the carriage in a different direction and drove through the now empty streets out of the City to where the *Palazzo* Sogino stood on high ground surrounded by its gardens and trees.

As he approached it, Lord Mere found his heart beating with excitement not only because he had saved Florencia, but also because he would see her.

He found it hard to believe he had been so successful and that it was not a question of being frustrated and having to try again.

The film and the prints were in his tail-coat pocket and Vincente was dead.

He reasoned that since the Prince's body-guard was out of the way and the garden of the West Tower was at the opposite end of the house from the rooms occupied by his father, it might be morning before his body was discovered.

There would obviously be a great deal of consternation, but it was unlikely to be suspected immediately that he had been killed by another man.

As those who lived with him must have been well aware, he both drank and took drugs, and it would therefore be assumed at first, at any rate, that he had fallen over the ramparts without there being any question of foul play.

Only the young cousin might reveal that there had been some sort of fight between him and a man whom she could not identify.

But even if that all came to light tomorrow, Lord Mere reasoned, the pride of the Gorizias would not wish to admit that the Prince had been vanquished in a fight, or murdered by some unknown assailant.

It would be far more dignified to have it announced that he had died of a heart-attack or perhaps following an accident which had left him unconscious in the night air with the result that he had developed pneumonia.

He was well aware that the Florentine aristocrats were so proud that it would be imperative for them to hide from the world anything that belittled one of their number in any way.

He could therefore be almost certain that

Prince Vincente's death would be reported in the most unsensational terms possible.

The carriage came to a standstill outside the arched gateway which was the entrance to the *Palazzo*.

When the footman rapped on the door it was opened by a surprised servant, obviously a young man who had not often been on night-duty and was not quite certain what to do about visitors who arrived at such a late hour.

Lord Mere got out of the carriage as soon as the door opened and said:

'I have to see Her Highness the Princess Florencia immediately! Will you kindly inform her I am here and ask her to speak with me?'

The man looked indecisive, then said:

'Her Highness is in the Chapel, M'Lord, but I'll give her your message.'

Lord Mere thought that was what he might have guessed and he said quickly:

'No, I will go to her myself! Stay where you are!'

He spoke with a note of authority in his voice and the servant did not question it.

Lord Mere turned and walked swiftly along the passages that were darkly shadowed and lit only by an occasional gas-globe, or more frequently by a candle in a silver sconce.

He knew where the Chapel was, because the Prince had shown it to him on their tour of inspection, for him to admire the carved reredos which framed an exceptionally beautiful picture by Taddeo Gaddi of the Crucifixion.

As Lord Mere reached the door he found it ajar, and saw that the Chapel was lit only by a number of candles burning at the front of the statues of the Saints, and by the light in the Sanctuary.

It was however, easy to distinguish the slim figure of Florencia with her golden hair hidden by a black lace veil, kneeling on the Chancel steps in front of the altar.

Lord Mere knew that she was praying for him and he felt a thrill of gratitude that he had found when he had least expected it, somebody so perfect so completely what he wanted as his wife.

He knew that no other woman of

his acquaintance, or of those who had professed their love for him, would be kneeling at this hour of the night in prayer on his behalf.

Quietly, making little sound with his feet on the thick carpet which ran the length of the centre aisle, he walked forward until he reached Florencia.

She was concentrating so deeply on the prayer she was sending up to Heaven that her head was thrown back a little, her hands were clasped palm to palm in the age-old attitude of prayer, and her eyes were closed.

He thought as he looked at her that only Raphael could have depicted her as she was, looking like Mary hearing the Annunciation, and pleading with her body, heart and soul as she prayed.

Then as Lord Mere knelt down beside Florencia she was suddenly aware of him, and he felt a tremor run through her as if she came back to earth from the sky.

Slowly she turned her head to look at him.

Their eyes met, and in a low voice

which was deep and moved because of the sanctity of the place they were in and because she was sacred too, Lord Mere said:

'Your prayers, my darling, have been answered!'

For a moment she stared at him incredulously.

Then as the tears came into her eyes she whispered:

'You mean...?'

'Your father is safe and so are you!'

She looked at him for a moment, then turned her head as it had been before, shut her eyes and as her lips moved silently Lord Mere knew she was expressing her gratitude to the Power that had helped them.

He too said a quick prayer, at the same time making a note in his mind that on his return to England he would give a thanks offering to the Church which would express what he felt far more effectively than he could do in words.

Then as he rose to his feet Florencia rose too.

After she had genuflected to the altar she slipped her hand into his, and they walked from the Chapel side by side.

There was a Sitting-Room opposite the Chapel which also contained some fine pictures, and as Florencia opened the door Lord Mere saw that it was lit only by a fire that was still burning in the huge fireplace.

He guessed it was where the family had been sitting earlier in the evening, but for the moment all he was concerned with was Florencia.

As he put his arms around her she melted against him, saying in a hesitating little voice:

'Is it true..is it really true..that you have..saved Papa?'

'I have saved you both!'

Then his lips were on hers and he kissed her passionately, demandingly, until he felt as though they were both in a cloudless sky and there were no more problems to frighten them.

Only when he raised his head did Florencia whisper:

'I..I cannot believe it! Are you..sure that..Vincente will make no more..demands upon us?'

Lord Mere drew in his breath.

Then knowing that there was still a great deal more to do before they were completely 'out of the wood', he said:

'I must speak to your father, my darling, and as there is very little time for everything that has to be done, I think you must take me to him now, even though I want to stay here kissing you for the rest of tonight!'

He felt a little tremor run through her at his words and he pulled her against him saying:

'I love you! God, how I love you! But there are still things to be done, and however difficult it may be, I must not kiss you again until you know what my plans are.'

She knew he was speaking seriously and he loved the way she accepted what he had said without argument.

Instead she put out her hand to draw him from the room saying as she did so:

'Papa has gone to bed. But because he is

so worried, I suspect he will be sitting up in front of the fire as he does every evening because he finds it impossible to sleep.'

Lord Mere did not reply. He merely let Florencia lead him down the shadowy passages and up a staircase which led, he knew, to the private apartments of the family.

They stopped in front of an impressive door on which Florencia knocked gently, and when there was no reply she opened it.

She walked into a large room with a huge four-poster bed at the far end of it which Lord Mere saw at a quick glance was unoccupied.

Sitting in a high-backed armchair in front of the dying fire was the Prince, and although there was a newspaper on his knees he was in fact asleep.

Florencia moved towards him, and even before she reached him and spoke the Prince's head came up with a jerk and he said:

'I was just dozing. What do you want, my dearest?'

'Lord Mere is here, Papa, and he has something to tell you.'

The Prince sat upright, and Lord Mere followed Florencia across the room.

He saw the Prince was wearing a heavy velvet robe over his silk night-shirt and even dressed as he was, he looked very distinguished.

There were however dark lines of anxiety and hopelessness round his eyes, and the hand he held out to Lord Mere trembled.

'Forgive me if I do not get up to greet you, My Lord,' he said courteously.

'I must apologise for calling at such a late hour,' Lord Mere replied, 'but I have something to give you which I think you have been wanting for some time.'

As he spoke, he drew from the pocket of his tail-coat the prints and the film which he had taken from the safe in Vincente's bedroom.

He handed them to the Prince who stared at them incredulously, and Florencia giving a little cry went down on her knees beside her father's chair.

Then she looked up at Lord Mere and

he saw the tears that were running down her cheeks.

'How can you have done anything so incredible..so wonderful as to bring these to us?' she cried.

The Prince was still staring down in a dazed manner at what he held in his hands, and Lord Mere said:

'May I suggest, Your Highness, that you throw them immediately into the fire then we can all of us forget that they ever existed.'

The Prince did not speak and he went on:

'I think some of the prints do not concern you, as I brought from the safe everything that was there. But they too and the films should be destroyed so that when Prince Vincente's victims learn of his death they will know that they are free.'

'Vincente is dead?'

The Prince spoke for the first time since Lord Mere had given him the prints and the words seemed to ring out almost like a pistol-shot.

'He is dead!' Lord Mere repeated. 'I

think there is every likelihood his death will not be discovered until far later in the night, or perhaps not until tomorrow morning.'

He paused before he said:

'I want Your Highness to understand that in the circumstances it would be far the best from Florencia's point of view if when the news is broken you have already left Florence.'

The Prince drew in his breath, but his voice was quite calm and steady as he asked:

'Where do you wish us to go?'

'I want you to rouse the household and inform them that you have received news that a close relative, or perhaps a very dear friend of the family, is critically ill in Paris,' Lord Mere replied. 'Then you, Florencia and, if you wish it, Prince Antonio will leave on the first train for France.'

'And when we reach Paris?'

Lord Mere smiled.

'When you do so, I do not wish you to stay there but to go immediately to England, where I would like you to be my guests in my house in Oxfordshire.'

He looked at Florencia as he said:

'It is there that Florencia and I can be married very quietly, and later, when all the excitement and chatter there will be over Prince Vincente's death has died down, our marriage can be announced to the world.'

With a look of surprise on his face the Prince listened to what Lord Mere had to say. Then he turned towards Florencia to ask:

'Is this what you want, my dear?'

'Oh, yes, Papa! I love him, and now that Vincente is dead there is no reason for me not to say so.'

The Prince did not reply. He merely rose to his feet and taking the prints and the films he threw them into the fire.

The moment they touched the dying embers the celluloid burst into flames and the light from it illuminated the whole room.

Lord Mere's eyes were on Florencia, and as he lifted her to her feet she turned and hid her face against his shoulder.

'It is all over,' he said quietly, 'and now I must leave you and go back to the Villa. I will leave immediately on the first available train, before yours if possible, for it would be a mistake, as you will understand, for us to travel together.'

He looked down at her then continued:

'I shall however be waiting for you in Paris, and from there we will proceed to England where, as quickly as possible, you will become my wife.'

He felt her body tremble with what he knew was excitement.

Then as she looked at him the tears welled up in her eyes and as her cheeks became wet with them Lord Mere thought that no woman could be more lovely or more entrancing.

They just looked at each other, and the Prince turned from where he had been contemplating the flames which were destroying the false evidence against him and said:

'I do not know, My Lord, how I can ever thank you.'

'I can answer that very easily,' Lord Mere said. 'I want Florencia to be mine and I would also be very grateful if you will follow and will bring to England with you the Florentine necklace. It will cause my sister great distress if her husband realises she has lost it.'

'I can only apologise...' the Prince began humbly.

'No, please,' Lord Mere interrupted, 'there is no need. I understand perfectly the circumstances, Your Highness, that made it imperative for your son to retrieve the necklace. But now I suggest that before you leave you instruct Giovanni to make an exact copy of the necklace.'

'Copy it?' the Prince asked in a puzzled voice.

'When he has done so, we will give the copy to my sister, and I am certain my brother-in-law will not have the slightest idea it is not the original, while the one that means so much to your family can then be restored to its proper place.'

The Prince drew in his breath.

'There are no words in which to thank

you for your kindness.'

'I will ask Florencia to do that,' Lord Mere said with a smile, 'if you will permit her to accompany me to the carriage which is waiting for me below, while you make all the arrangements necessary to leave as quickly as possible. It is unnecessary for me to emphasise that it must appear as if you had left Florence before you had any idea that Prince Vincente was dead.'

The Prince nodded.

'Yes, of course. I will do exactly as you say.'

He put out his hand as he spoke and Lord Mere shook it.

Then he drew Florencia from the room, aware as he did so that the Prince was already tugging the bell-rope to summon his valet.

Lord Mere walked with Florencia back along the passage which led to the main staircase, and just before they reached it he stopped and taking her in his arms he kissed her until both their heart were beating violently.

212

Now he knew she belonged to him completely.

'I..love you!' Florencia whispered. 'I love you..and no one could be..more clever..or more..marvellous!'

She gave a little laugh that was half a sob as she said:

'I told you that not even..St. George..St. Michael..or all the angels could..save me..but you have done it and now I want to kneel at your feet in gratitude!'

'I would rather hold you in my arms,' Lord Mere said and his voice was deep with feeling. 'I adore you, my little Madonna, and now there are no longer any barriers to prevent me from telling you so, and as it will take me a lifetime, the sooner we are married the better!'

'I..I hope Papa will not expect us to..wait,' Florencia said, 'but our relatives might be..shocked!'

'That is why our marriage will be kept a secret,' Lord Mere said. 'We will spend a long time in England, and after Prince Vincente's death is announced nobody will be particularly surprised.'

'I..I hope you are right,' Florencia said doubtfully. 'I want to be married to you..I want to be with you..but I would not wish..for your sake as well as ours..for there to be any..scandal.'

'Leave everything to me,' Lord Mere replied. 'Our faith and our prayers, my darling, have brought us already so much happiness that I do not believe they will fail us now.'

He kissed her again.

Then, as if he could hardly bear to tear himself away, he left her at the top of the stairs and ran down to where the night-footman stood with the door open.

He stepped into his carriage, and as he drove back to the Villa he was planning exactly how he would have a private coach attached to the train from Paris to the coast so that he could be with Florencia and the Prince on the last lap of their journey.

What was important was that he should leave before they did, and he knew that by the time he reached the Villa, Hicks would have had all his things packed and found out what time the first train left.

It all seemed to fit into place like a rather intricate puzzle, but which to his utter relief no longer puzzled him.

He realised that he had not only done exactly what the Earl of Rosebery had asked him to do, but had also found Florencia for himself and saved her from a hell which no woman should be expected to endure.

He knew that he was the luckiest and most fortunate of men and to his own surprise he found himself saying:

'Thank you, God, thank you!'

★ ★ ★ ★

As Lord Mere had anticipated, Hicks was waiting for him and he saw as he entered his bedroom in the Villa that his boxes were already packed and his travelling-clothes were laid out on a chair.

With a faint smile on his lips he started to take off his evening-coat saying:

'What time are we leaving, Hicks!'

'I've ordered the carriage, M'Lord, for five o'clock, an' I've told all them prepared to listen that you've been informed by a Queen's Messenger that the Queen requires your presence urgently.'

'Thank you, Hicks. You did splendidly,' Lord Mere replied, 'and what is important is that everybody at the *Contessa's* party believed you!'

He knew there was a smile of gratification on Hicks' lips, but he merely said:

'I've enjoyed our adventure in Florence, M'Lord! Makes a change from the humdrum monotony of everyday life at home, so to speak.'

'I think, however, this will be our last adventure,' Lord Mere replied, thinking of Florencia.

'I doubts it!' Hicks said. 'If it ain't one thing, it'll be another!'

Lord Mere did not reply. He merely looked amused.

He wondered what Hicks would feel when he learnt he was to marry.

There might even be a feeling of jealousy, for Hicks was very possessive.

Although he supposed it was really a vast impertinence, Lord Mere was aware that Hicks always seemed somewhat contemptuous of the women in his life.

It was as if he knew they had no right there, and anyway, would not last very long.

Now as he got into bed he thought over the position.

When Florencia was his, there would, in the words of the old song, be 'no need to go a-roaming'.

He could think of nothing more wonderful than for them to be together in the peace and quiet of the countryside around his house.

'She is everything I have always wanted,' he told himself.

Her lovely face was vivid in his mind's eye, and he asked how it was possible in so short a space of time that she should fill his whole existence to the exclusion of everything else.

Although he thought of himself as an

adventurer he had always been sure that he was completely master of his own soul.

While women had amused him and he could not imagine his life without them, they were always dispensable, and none of his love-affairs ever lasted very long.

But he knew now that this was because something had always been missing.

Although he shied from admitting it, he knew now their attraction had been merely physical, and there had been nothing spiritual in his feelings towards any woman until he had met Florencia.

When he thought it over, he came to the conclusion that the feelings that had been aroused in him by the pictures that he loved and the beauty he sought in everything in fact sprang from the spiritual side of his nature.

But he had never been able to share this with anybody else.

Now he knew that this too was so much a part of Florencia that they were joined by an invisible bond which would hold them linked to one another for all eternity.

'I love her!' he said aloud.

He knew then that the words for the first time in his life, had the real meaning which involved both the physical and spiritual side of his heart and especially the latter.

It was Raphael who had made him aware of what he sought in the woman he would marry, although he had not previously expressed it in so many words even to himself.

Now he knew that only his desire for perfection had prevented him from accepting 'second-best' because had been quite certain he would never find his ideal.

But now he had found her, and in strange and extraordinary circumstances which had even involved the death of a man who deserved to die.

He felt no guilt about killing Vincente, for even though he had not intended to kill him, he had in fact rid the world of a man who had hurt and ruined perhaps hundreds of people in one way or another.

His death had also saved a great number

of young and innocent victims from his bestiality.

'He must be forgotten,' Lord Mere decided.

He hoped that once she was away from Florence Florencia would forget the horror of what she had lived through and so would her father.

Just as the falsely incriminating evidence was now turned to ashes, so in the years to come the wickedness and licentiousness of Vincente would vanish into the darkness of the past as other villains had vanished before him.

Everything he was, everything he had done, was as much part of Florence as was its beauty and its culture.

And yet when one thought of the glorious City, all one remembered was the good, and not the bad.

Lord Mere knew that his task now was to make the woman he loved forget.

Just as he had planned how he would lift her into a world where there was only the light of angels.

And of course Love.

7

Florencia stood at the window looking out at the English countryside.

She had had no idea that the grass in England could be so green or that the lake that lay just beyond the terrace would be so beautiful with black and white swans moving serenely on its silver surface.

In the park under the huge, ancient oak trees there were spotted deer, and as she watched a flight of white doves flew from the trees towards the house.

She felt as if she had been in a dream ever since Lord Mere had arrived at the *Palazzo* late that night to tell her that her father was free and so was she.

Every moment since then she had found herself thanking God for sending him into her life and thinking too that no man could be more wonderful.

When he left her pulsating from his

kisses she had felt a flood of excitement sweep over her and had run as quickly as she could to wake her brother.

He was sleeping in the room where Lord Mere had come to her by climbing up the wall.

She burst in through the door and groping her way in the darkness towards the bed she cried out:

'Wake up, Antonio! Wake up! We are leaving for England!'

Now she felt Antonio stir and wonder what was happening.

'Listen, Antonio,' she said, 'you must hurry and I have something important to tell you!'

Her brother was now sitting up and lighting a candle beside his bed.

As it flickered into light he turned to look at his sister in astonishment.

'What are you talking about? Did you say we are to leave for England?'

'Lord Mere has saved Papa and me, and Vincente is dead!'

For a moment it seemed as if Prince Antonio's breath was taken away by what he had heard.

Then he exclaimed:

'Is that possible? Are you sure of what you are saying?'

'Quite, quite sure!' Florencia replied. 'Lord Mere has brought Papa the incriminating evidence and the negatives from which the prints were taken. They are burnt and nobody can ever blackmail him again!'

'I can hardly believe it!'

'It is true! It is true!' Florencia replied, 'and because Vincente is dead we must leave Florence before it is announced. So hurry, Antonio! Papa is alerting the servants and telling them we have to leave at once for Paris because somebody close to us is extremely ill!'

'I feel bewildered by what you are saying,' Antonio complained, pushing his dark hair back from his forehead.

'I know it all sounds like a fairy story,' Florencia agreed, 'but we can talk about it later. Just get dressed and tell your valet to pack everything you require.'

She walked towards the door and as she

reached it she warned him:

'Remember to tell the servants that we are going to Paris. But actually Lord Mere is taking us to England to stay at his house in Oxfordshire.'

She did not wait for her brother to reply, but ran to her father's room.

She found him there already half-dressed, while his valet, summoned by the bell, was packing his trunk in an adjoining room.

Before Florencia could speak, her father's Major Domo who ran the household for him came hurrying along the passage obviously perturbed by the commotion.

It was to him that the Prince gave instructions that a groom was to ride immediately to Giovanni's private house and bring back a parcel.

The Prince sat down at his *secretaire* in the corner of his bedroom as he spoke and hastily wrote a note to Giovanni which Florencia knew contained instructions to make a sketch of the necklace as Lord Mere had suggested and to give the groom the original.

She knew Giovanni would have the necklace in a private safe in his own house since because of its great value it would be dangerous to leave it in his shop on the Ponte Vecchio at night.

Only Lord Mere, she thought, could set so many wheels in motion and be certain that they would work as efficiently as he apparently planned his own life.

She was even more certain that this was so when they reached Paris, only a few hours after Lord Mere himself had arrived there, to find him waiting to transfer them to the Gare du Nord, where his private carriage had been attached to the boat-train for Calais.

Because they had all been tired after a sleepless night not only Florencia but her father and brother had slept intermittently in the train from Florence.

But by the time she arrived in Paris and saw Lord Mere Florencia felt she was so happy and loved him so much that she could fly in the sky or dance on the silver waters of the Seine.

He saw as he helped her from the train

that her face was radiant.

When their hands touched, their vibrations joined one with the other's, and he had the feeling that even marriage could not make them any closer than they were already.

The sun was shining in Paris and the tall houses with their grey shutters and the chestnut trees in blossom were very attractive.

As Florencia looked around her eagerly Lord Mere whispered:

'I will bring you back here one day soon, and you will find that Paris is a City made for love and laughter.'

She felt herself quiver at the way he spoke, and when her eyes looked into his she thought it would not matter where they were, so long as they were together.

They would find love and laughter, and many other wonderful things as well.

Because Lord Mere did not want Florencia to be too tired they did not cross the Channel that night but stayed in a comfortable Château on the outskirts of Calais.

It belonged to an elderly couple who had been friends of his father and they immediately found they had a great deal in common with the Prince.

Antonio tactfully made himself scarce and Lord Mere was able to take Florencia into the Conservatory ostensibly to look at the flowers.

The moment they were alone together he said:

'My darling, I have not had an opportunity until now to tell you how beautiful you are and how happy I am that all your troubles are over.'

'I have been wondering how I can ever find..words in which to..thank you,' Florencia replied in a low voice.

'I do not want you to do that,' Lord Mere said. 'All I want is never again to see the look of fear in your eyes which was there when we first met.'

'Now I am no longer afraid,' she answered, 'but I know, if ever I am, I shall only have to tell you about it.'

It was not only what she said but the radiance in her eyes as she raised her face to his that made him pull her against him and look down at her for a long moment before he said:

'You are perfect, my Madonna, for whom I have been searching all my life! I never believed I would find you, except in a picture on a wall.'

'I am..real,' Florencia said softly.

'I will make sure of that!' Lord Mere answered.

His lips found hers and he kissed her until he could feel her heart beating frantically against his, and knew that never in his life had he known anything so rapturous as the sensations she aroused in him.

Yet because he knew the Prince would not approve of their staying too long in the Conservatory, they returned to their hosts and retired to bed early.

★ ★ ★ ★

The next day they crossed the Channel and found waiting for them at Dover, Lord Mere's private train which was to carry them to Mere Park.

Florencia had never been in a private train before and she felt it was as exciting as having a doll's house of her own.

She explored it with an excitement which made Lord Mere smile at her tenderly.

'I adore you when you behave like a child!' he said so that only she could hear. 'Until now you have always been a very serious, troubled young woman. But now you are very different.'

'Very, very different, thanks to you!' Florencia whispered.

'But even then I found you entrancing,' Lord Mere smiled.

At the same time he knew, as he had said, that he adored her now that she looked young and carefree, no longer overshadowed by tragedy and danger as she had been when they first met.

Every moment they were together he thought he loved her more.

He looked forward with an almost boyish enthusiasm to showing her his home and the places in the garden and on the estate which had meant so much to him all his life.

It was, however, quite late when they arrived at Mere Park, and after diner Lord Mere had suggested that the Prince should retire, and also Florencia.

When they had gone upstairs Antonio had lingered behind and Lord Mere realised he wished to speak to him.

'What is it, Antonio?' he asked.

After a moment's hesitation the young man said:

'I wanted to ask you—do you think your sister will ever forgive me?'

'I have been thinking about that myself,' Lord Mere admitted. 'If it does not embarrass you too much, the only member of my family I would like to have at my wedding, which we have all agreed must be very secret, is my sister Jennifer.'

'Perhaps she will understand why I— behaved as I did when she hears the—whole story,' Antonio said hesitantly.

'I am sure she will,' Lord Mere said to comfort him. 'Tomorrow I intend to talk to your father about my marriage to Florencia and make arrangements for it to take place as soon as possible.'

He did not say any more at the time, but he had the perceptive feeling that although the Prince was overwhelmingly grateful for what he had done for them, he might still have reservations about his daughter marrying a man who was not a Catholic.

Therefore, the following morning he was not particularly surprised when the Prince asked to speak to him alone, and when breakfast was finished Lord Mere took him into his Study.

'As I am sure you will understand,' the Prince began, 'all I want is my daughter's happiness. We are most deeply in your debt, but you must be aware that we are a Catholic family. For any marriage that takes place, especially in families as old as ours, it is considered obligatory by the Church that we insist on the children that may result from the union being brought up as Catholics.'

It was what Lord Mere had expected and he said:

'I am aware of that, Your Highness, and

I have what I think is a solution to that problem, as well as to the others with which you have already confronted me. It is one that was solved fifty years ago when my grandfather married the *Contesse* Marie-Thérèse de Beauchamp, whose family in France was as respected and revered as yours is in Italy.'

The Prince was listening intently as Lord Mere went on:

'My grandmother was of course a Catholic, and my grandfather, the fourth Lord Mere, was very proud that the Meres have supported the Protestant cause ever since one of my ancestors had been at the Court of King Henry VIII.'

He smiled before he said:

'It seemed incredible at the time that my grandfather should wish to marry a Roman Catholic, but in fact he fell deeply in love with the young *Contesse* Marie-Thérèse, in the same way that I love Florencia.'

'What happened?' the Prince asked.

'They reached a compromise both between themselves and with their spiritual instructors,' Lord Mere replied. 'Any daughters of the marriage would be brought up as Catholics, the boys would be Protestants.'

'And that proved acceptable to both Churches?'

'Apparently it did,' Lord Mere replied. 'My grandfather and grandmother had six children—an equal number of boys and girls—and they were so happy that they became almost a legend not only in the family, but also in the countryside.'

The Prince gave a short laugh.

'Once again, Ingram, you have removed a heavy burden from my shoulders. With such a precedent I feel it would be impossible for anybody to criticise me for allowing a marriage which might not have the approval of the Church.'

'That is what I hoped you would think,' Lord Mere said, 'and because I know it would make you happy, we will be married not here in my Chapel, but in a small Catholic Church at the far end of my estate where I hope we can keep the ceremony a secret.'

He smiled before he added:

'In fact, I am sure that even the local villagers will not be aware it is I who am the bridegroom.'

Lord Mere, with his brilliance at organisation, intended to make sure of this by keeping the doors of the Church locked and arranging for the local people to be told that the marriage was between two foreigners.

As far as he was concerned, the God who had helped him save Florencia from the horrors of a marriage with a man like Vincente was the same as the one to whom she prayed.

He knew the prayers which had come from the depths of their hearts had been answered because good had triumphed over evil.

All that mattered was that Florencia should be his wife, and he knew that together they would shut out of their lives all that was bestial and depraved and try as far as was humanly possible to spread their happiness around them.

As he became conscious of what he was thinking, he realised it was strangely different from the way he had looked at life since growing up.

He knew that Florencia had not only brought him the realisation of his dreams, but her personality had raised in him new aspirations and ideals that he had never known before.

★ ★ ★ ★

The following morning Lord Mere left very early for London.

He carried with him the necklace that the Prince had given him as soon as they arrived at Mere Park.

'I sent a note to Giovanni, as you suggested,' the Prince said, 'and before he handed the necklace to my servant, he made a drawing of it so that he could start work on it immediately and make the replica you have asked for.'

Lord Mere nodded agreement and the Prince said tentatively:

'I am afraid it will be very expensive!'

'That is of no consequence,' Lord Mere replied, 'I know it will make you all happy to know that the necklace is returned to its proper place and will be there for Antonio to hand down to his children.'

The Prince was very moved and put his hand on Lord Mere's shoulder.

'I thank God every day in my prayers that we ever met you,' he said quietly.

Lord Mere reached London at nine o'clock and drove immediately to his brother-in-law's house in Park Lane.

As he expected, he was told on arrival that Her Ladyship was not yet up, but His Lordship was in the Dining-Room.

For a moment Lord Mere considered saying he would go straight to his sister's bedroom. Then he thought that would be a mistake.

Instead he went into the Dining-Room where the Marquess was having breakfast with a dozen silver *entrée* dishes arranged on a side-board.

He looked up in surprise at Lord Mere and exclaimed:

'Good gracious, Ingram! I was not expecting you! I heard you were abroad.'

'I have just returned,' Lord Mere said,

'and I want to see Jennie.'

'She is still in bed,' the Marquess replied. 'Sit down and have something to eat.'

Out of politeness more than the fact that he was hungry, Lord Mere helped himself from one of the dishes on the side-board and accepted a cup of coffee that was poured out for him by the Butler.

'Was your visit to Paris successful?' he asked.

He knew as he spoke that the Marquess would give him a voluble, lengthy and undoubtedly somewhat boring account of his visit.

He was not mistaken and when at length he came to the end the Marquess added:

'I was very tired by the time I returned home. I am getting too old for all these visits abroad, the long discussions and the even longer meals they entail!'

Lord Mere looked at him in surprise.

'Are you not well, Arthur?' he enquired.

'I have not yet told your sister,' the Marquess replied, 'but I saw my Physician on my return and he has warned me that my heart is not in good shape.'

'I am sorry to hear that!'

'He has advised me to take things easy, but my position at Court makes that difficult.'

'You must tell Her Majesty the truth.'

'If I do, I doubt if she will listen,' the Marquess said grimly. 'Like all women when she wants something Her Majesty expects one to obey and at the double!'

'I am sure that is true,' Lord Mere smiled, 'but it would be a mistake to take risks, and I am sure Jennie would tell you so too.'

'I do not think I will even mention it to her,' the Marquess said. 'Personally, I find ill-health a bore and do not want to talk about it.'

Lord Mere drank his coffee and rose from the table.

'I will go up and see Jennie now,' he said. 'I am sorry to hear what you have told me, Arthur. My advice is to refuse to take on anything which you think is too much for you.'

But Lord Mere knew as he left the

room that his brother-in-law would not listen to him.

He enjoyed his position of power in Court Circles, and Lord Mere had the feeling that he would do his duty, however much it cost him, to the end of his life.

When Lord Mere walked into his sister's bedroom he was struck even more than he had been in the past by the vast difference in age there was between his sister and her husband.

Jennie had obviously not been awake long, but she looked very fresh and young with her hair falling over her shoulders and her pink-and-white complexion clear in the sunlight which seemed also to be caught in her eyes when she saw who her visitor was.

'Ingram!' she exclaimed. 'You are back! Oh, dearest, I have been thinking about you!'

'As I have been thinking about you,' Lord Mere said.

He put the package he was carrying in his hand down in front of her on the sheet.

For a moment she did not touch it, but looked at it fearfully as if she did not dare to believe what she hoped.

'Is it..is it really..?' she faltered.

'It is your necklace!' Lord Mere said sitting down on the side of the bed.

'Oh, Ingram, you have brought it back to me!'

The tears were in her eyes as she held out both hands to him saying:

'How can you have been so clever? How can I ever thank you?'

Lord Mere kissed her, then glanced across the room to make sure that the door was shut.

'I have a long story to tell you, Jennie, about the necklace and why it was taken from you.'

Her eyes dropped before his and the colour rose in her cheeks, and he knew she felt embarrassed at remembering what had happened.

Very quietly Lord Mere told her the whole story of what had occurred since his leaving for Florence on her behalf.

As he spoke Jennie's eyes were raised

to his, and as she listened to the whole extraordinary story her eyes seemed to grow wider and wider until they filled her whole face.

Only when he told her how he had brought the Soginos back with him and that the Prince, Florencia and Antonio were now at Mere Park did she give a little gasp.

'They..are here..in England?'

'It was essential that they should get away before the announcement of Vincente's death,' Lord Mere said, 'and also I intend to marry Florencia as soon as possible.'

'Marry her?' Jennie exclaimed.

'I have fallen in love,' Lord Mere explained quietly, 'and I do not intend to wait while she pretends to mourn a man who should have been killed years ago for his crimes against young girls.'

'And you say it must be a secret marriage?'

'Just for the time being,' Lord Mere said. 'You will be the only member of our family who will know what has happened for at least three months!'

He paused before he added:

'That is why I am asking you to come home with me this evening or, if you prefer, tomorrow. Florencia and I will be married on Thursday.'

Jennie did not answer for a moment. Then she said:

'You know, Ingram, dearest, I want you to be happy, but I am..shy at the thought of meeting..Antonio.'

'As he is shy of meeting you,' Lord Mere said. 'That is why, if you can arrange it, I think it would be best for you to come back with me this evening. Then you can have all tomorrow to make explanations to one another before creating a further problem for me and upsetting my wedding day.'

Jennie laughed.

'Oh, dearest, of course I would not wish to do that!'

She hesitated for a moment. Then she said:

'Actually, I feel so much happier now that I know the real reason why Antonio took the necklace! I had felt so ashamed and..humiliated to think that he had..made up to me simply because he was a..thief!'

She did not have to say any more. Lord Mere understood exactly what she was feeling.

When they travelled back together later in the day, he knew that the sudden silences between them and the look on her face when they reached Mere Park were due to her feeling as shy as any young girl might be on encountering her lover again.

But they had both underestimated the tact and charm of the Italians.

Antonio greeted Jennie so naturally and unaffectedly that it swept away her embarrassment, and after she had been introduced to the Prince and Florencia he made some excuse to take her out through the open French window of the Drawing Room onto the terrace.

Lord Mere had not missed the expression in Antonio's eyes when he saw Jennie, and when a little later they came back into the Drawing Room and they all had a glass of champagne before going upstairs to dress for dinner, he thought he had never seen his sister look so pretty or so radiant.

It was for the first time an idea came to him which was to be substantiated later in the evening.

They had finished dinner and had sat down to talk over their precipitate journey from Florence.

Florencia had told Jennie how thrilled she had been to travel in Lord Mere's train, and looking at Jennie, Lord Mere thought at that moment she looked no older than Florencia.

Then the two girls went hand-in-hand up the stairs together alone.

The Prince followed them soon afterwards leaving Antonio with Lord Mere.

'You will have a drink before you go to bed?' Lord Mere asked.

'No, thank you,' Antonio replied. 'But there is something I wish to say to you.'

'What is that?'

It seemed for a moment as if the young Prince was finding it difficult to put his feelings into words.

Then Lord Mere prompted him by saying:

'Is it about Jennie?'

'You may think it is too soon,' the Prince said, 'and you may of course disapprove, but I love your sister, and I know she loves me too.'

For a moment Lord Mere was startled.

It was what he had suspected, but did not anticipate it would be put so bluntly.

'I have decided that however long it takes, I am going to wait for Jennie. I know her husband is far older than she is. Perhaps fate will be as kind to me as it has to you,' Antonio said, 'and one day we will be able to be together.'

The way he spoke with an undeniable note of sincerity in his voice was very moving and Lord Mere said:

'I love my sister, and I can only hope that she will be permitted to be as happy as I am.'

'Thank you,' Antonio replied. 'I do not want you to think I would do anything wrong behind your back, but Jennie has told me that she has not lived a normal married life with her husband for some years, which means that I do not feel I am in any way behaving wrongly in telling her of my love.'

'I can only say again that I hope you will both find happiness,' Lord Mere said.

When he went upstairs to bed he went first to his sister's room to say goodnight to her.

Once again he thought as he had this morning how young she looked.

As he sat down on the bed to take her hand in his he knew that the Marquess had left her unawakened to the joys and glory of love.

He did not speak for a moment and her eyes were on his face. He knew she was wondering what Antonio had said to him.

Then she asked in a low voice:

'Are you..shocked, Ingram?'

'No, of course not,' he said. 'All I want is for you to be as happy as Florencia and I will be.'

Jennie gave a little cry.

Then there were tears running down

her face, and she was kissing Lord Mere over and over again as if it was the only way she could express her gratitude and happiness.

★ ★ ★ ★

When Lord Mere and Florencia drove away on their honeymoon he felt that he had tied up all the problems and left everything neat and tidy for his return.

He was taking Florencia to a Hunting Lodge he owned in Leicestershire where he intended they should stay for the first part of their honeymoon.

He would then take her to another house that belonged to him and was situated in Cornwall.

He felt it would be a mistake to expect her to travel too long a distance after all she had been through in Florence.

He was driving a team of four of his finest horses and his chaise seemed almost to fly over the ground.

They had been married in the small Catholic Church which Lord Mere thought would have looked very unattractive if he had not had it massed with lilies.

But there were so many that they hid the bare walls, the rather ugly pillars, and made the whole place a bower of beauty.

He thought that the white lilies were a perfect symbol of Florencia when she became his wife.

As there had been no time to order an elaborate wedding gown, hers was very simple, but she wore over it the very exquisite fine Brussels lace veil that had been in the Mere family for generations.

On her head she carried a glittering diamond tiara which was part of the collection of family jewels, though Lord Mere felt it would have been more appropriate if it had been shaped as a halo.

She looked so lovely and so saint-like as the Prince brought her up the aisle that Lord Mere thought she should have been standing in one of the alcoves with candles burning below her.

The Service, because it was a mixed marriage, was a short one, but he knew that Florencia felt as if God blessed them through the Priest, as they had been blessed already.

They drove back to Mere Park where they toasted each other in champagne, and after a light luncheon Florencia changed and they drove off together with only Jennie and Antonio to shower them with rose petals.

'It was a lovely wedding!' Florencia said. 'Just the way I wanted to be married!'

'You are sure that is what you wanted?' Lord Mere asked. 'I was afraid you would miss having bridesmaids and a large congregation of admiring friends.'

'All I wanted was to be..alone with..you and..God,' Florencia said simply. 'And how did you guess that I love white lilies more than any other flower?'

'That is because you look like one,' Lord Mere replied, 'or rather, I thought when I saw you in Church that you looked like a Saint, and perhaps I should be worshipping you instead of marrying you!'

Florencia gave a little laugh, and laid her hand on his knee.

'I am not..really very saintly,' she said,
'and I know that..my love for you is
very..human.'

She said the words a little shyly and they
brought the fire into Lord Mere's eyes as
he said:

'I will teach you, my beautiful one, how
to be human when it is easier to touch you
than it is at the moment.'

Florencia gave a little sigh of happiness
and moved closer to him.

He thought as he drove on that no man
could be so happy and still be on earth.

★ ★ ★ ★

Later that night when the only light in
the room came from stars shining through
the uncurtained windows, Florencia with
her cheek against Lord Mere's shoulder
whispered:

'Do you..still love me?'

He drew her closer before he said:

'My darling, that is a ridiculous question!
If it should be asked at all, it is I who
should ask you.'

'You know that I love you,' Florencia said. 'I had no idea..until now..that love could be so..glorious..so exciting and so..wonderful!'

'That is what I want you to feel,' Lord Mere said, 'and it is what I have felt ever since I first met you.'

Florencia gave a deep sigh.

'How..when love is..like this could anybody marry without love?'

There was a little touch of horror in her voice which he did not miss.

'That is something,' he said, 'you are never to think about again! You are married to me and you love me as I love you.'

'I know,' Florencia said, 'and it has only been possible because you saved me and swept away everything that was dark and frightening..and which made me want..to die!'

'And what do you feel now?'

'I want to live and love you for a thousand years!'

He laughed before he said:

'That would not be long enough for me! We will be together for eternity, my precious, because we are no longer two people, but one, and nothing can ever divide us.'

Florencia gave a cry.

'Do you really believe that is true? I think it must be, because when I first met you I knew you were the man who had been in my dreams.'

'Just as I knew that I loved you in the portraits I had seen of you painted by Raphael nearly four hundred years ago, but I had no idea you were alive!'

'But..I am!' Florencia said.

His lips were very close to hers and his hand was moving over the softness of her body.

'You are quite certain you will not suddenly vanish?' he asked. 'You will not go back onto the canvas on the wall so that I shall be left yearning for you and finding every other woman disappointing because they are not you?'

'I am human! I am..human!'

The way Florencia spoke made his lips find hers and he kissed her at first very gently, as if she was infinitely precious.

Then as he felt her quiver against his body and he knew that he was awakening a little flame within her, his kiss became more insistent, more demanding.

When he released her lips Florencia said:

'I never guessed that..love was like..this!'

'Like what?'

'So..overwhelming..so strong and also like a..burning fire.'

'Real love is like nature itself,' Lord Mere said a little unsteadily, 'like the leaves on the trees, the snowy peaks of the mountains, and the deep green depths of the sea. It is also the burning sun which runs through our bodies like fire.'

'That is what..happens to me when you..kiss me,' Florencia whispered, 'and when you..love me the flames seem to..consume me completely so that I want to be part of you...'

Lord Mere drew in his breath.

Then he was kissing her again, kissing her until the fire blazed in them both.

He could feel her heart beating beneath his and knew that she wanted him as he wanted her and they were neither of them complete without the other.

Then, as the flames within them swept them up into the sky, they became one with the burning sun, while the stars still twinkled around them.

Lord Mere knew that he had found in the woman who belonged to him and who was his wife that he had sought, and which moved him so deeply, besides the faith which had guided him, inspired him, and helped him when he most needed it.

This was love in all its glory, the love that is eternal and which is life itself.

The publishers hope that this book has given you enjoyable reading. Large Print Books are especially designed to be as easy to see and hold as possible. If you wish a complete list of our books, please ask at your local library or write directly to: Magna Large Print Books, Long Preston, North Yorkshire, BD23 4ND, England.